About the Author

Agatha Christie is the most widely published author in any language, outsold only by the Bible. Her books have sold more than a billion copies in English and another hundred foreign languages. She is the author of eighty novels, short-story collections, around thirty plays, and six novels written under the name Mary Westmacott.

She first tried her hand at detective fiction while working in a hospital dispensary during World War I, creating the now legendary Hercule Poirot with her debut novel *The Mysterious Affair at Styles*. In 1930, Miss Jane Marple made her first full-length novel appearance in *The Murder at the Vicarage*, quickly becoming another beloved and enduring character to rival Poirot's popularity. Additional series characters include the husband-and-wife crime-fighting team of Tommy and Tuppence Beresford, private investigator Parker Pyne, and Scotland Yard detectives Superintendent Battle and Inspector Japp.

Many of Christie's novels and short stories were adapted into plays, films, and television series. *The Mousetrap* opened in 1952 and is the longest-running play in history. Academy Award-nominated actor and director Kenneth Branagh helmed the acclaimed major motion picture *Murder on the Orient Express* in 2017 and its sequel, *Death on the Nile*, starring as the Belgian detective. On the small screen Poirot has been most memorably portrayed by David Suchet, and Miss Marple by Joan Hickson and subsequently Geraldine McEwan and Julia McKenzie.

Christie was first married to Archibald Christie and then to archaeologist Sir Max Mallowan, whom she accompanied on expeditions to countries that would also serve as the settings for many of her novels. In 1971 she achieved one of Britain's highest honors when she was made a Dame of the British Empire. She died in 1976 at the age of eighty-five. The one-hundred-year anniversary of Agatha Christie stories and the debut of Hercule Poirot was celebrated around the world in 2020.

www.AgathaChristie.com

The Agatha Christie Collection

The Man in the Brown Suit
The Secret of Chimneys
The Seven Dials Mystery
The Mysterious Mr. Quin
The Sittaford Mystery
Parker Pyne Investigates
Why Didn't They Ask Evans?
Murder Is Easy
The Regatta Mystery and Other Stories
And Then There Were None
Towards Zero
Death Comes as the End
Sparkling Cyanide
The Witness for the Prosecution and
   Other Stories
Crooked House
Three Blind Mice and Other Stories
They Came to Baghdad
Destination Unknown
Ordeal by Innocence
Double Sin and Other Stories
The Pale Horse
Star over Bethlehem: Poems and
   Holiday Stories
Endless Night
Passenger to Frankfurt
The Golden Ball and Other Stories
The Mousetrap and Other Plays
The Harlequin Tea Set

The Hercule Poirot Mysteries

The Mysterious Affair at Styles
The Murder on the Links
Poirot Investigates
The Murder of Roger Ackroyd
The Big Four
The Mystery of the Blue Train
Peril at End House
Lord Edgware Dies
Murder on the Orient Express
Three Act Tragedy
Death in the Clouds
The A.B.C. Murders
Murder in Mesopotamia
Cards on the Table
Murder in the Mews
Dumb Witness
Death on the Nile

Appointment with Death
Hercule Poirot's Christmas
Sad Cypress
One, Two, Buckle My Shoe
Evil Under the Sun
Five Little Pigs
The Hollow
The Labors of Hercules
Taken at the Flood
The Under Dog and Other Stories
Mrs. McGinty's Dead
After the Funeral
Hickory Dickory Dock
Dead Man's Folly
Cat Among the Pigeons
The Clocks
Third Girl
Hallowe'en Party
Elephants Can Remember
Curtain: Poirot's Last Case

The Miss Marple Mysteries

The Murder at the Vicarage
The Body in the Library
The Moving Finger
A Murder Is Announced
They Do It with Mirrors
A Pocket Full of Rye
4:50 from Paddington
The Mirror Crack'd from Side to Side
A Caribbean Mystery
At Bertram's Hotel
Nemesis
Sleeping Murder
Miss Marple: The Complete
   Short Stories

The Tommy and Tuppence Mysteries

The Secret Adversary
Partners in Crime
N or M?
By the Pricking of My Thumbs
Postern of Fate

Memoirs

An Autobiography
Come, Tell Me How You Live

Agatha Christie

Star over
Bethlehem

Poems and Holiday Stories

Illustrations by Elise Wrigley

wm

WILLIAM MORROW
An Imprint of HarperCollins_Publishers_

STAR OVER BETHLEHEM © 1965. THE ROAD OF DREAMS © 1924. POEMS © 1973. Published by permission of G.P. Putnam's Sons, a member of Penguin Group (USA) Inc. All rights reserved. Printed in the United States of America. No part of this book may be used or reproduced in any manner whatsoever without written permission except in the case of brief quotations embodied in critical articles and reviews. For information, address HarperCollins Publishers, 195 Broadway, New York, NY 10007.

HarperCollins books may be purchased for educational, business, or sales promotional use. For information, please write: Special Markets Department, HarperCollins Publishers, 195 Broadway, New York, NY 10007.

For more information about educational use, teachers should visit www.HarperAcademic.com.

FIRST HARPER PAPERBACK PUBLISHED 2011.

Designed by Michael P. Correy

Library of Congress Cataloging-in-Publication Data is available upon request.

ISBN 978-0-06-207430-0

22 23 24 25 26   DIX/LSC   10 9 8 7 6 5 4 3

For Hydie

Contents

STAR OVER BETHLEHEM

A Greeting

Praise to the Yule Log!
    Leap, Flames, merrily.
Hail to the Wassail Bowl!
    Bubble, Wine, rosily!

In the Manger lies the Child;
Asses, Oxen, braying, lowing,
Cackling Hens and Cocks a'crowing.
Overfull the Inn to-night,
Up above a star shines bright,
Shepherds kneel beside their fold,
Wise Men bring their gifts of Gold,
Angels in the Sky above
Trumpet forth God's gift of Love.

Waken, children, one and all,
Wake to hear the trumpet call,
Leave your sleeping, 'tis the Day,
    Christmas, glorious Christmas Day!

Star over Bethlehem

Mary looked down at the baby in the manger. She was alone in the stable except for the animals. As she smiled down at the child her heart was full of pride and happiness.

Then suddenly she heard the rustling of wings and turning, she saw a great Angel standing in the doorway.

The Angel shone with the radiance of the morning sun, and the beauty of his face was so great that Mary's eyes were dazzled and she had to turn aside her head.

Then the Angel said (and his voice was like a golden trumpet): "Do not be afraid, Mary. . . ."

And Mary answered in her sweet low voice:

"I am not afraid, Oh Holy One of God, but the Light of your Countenance dazzles me."

The Angel said: "I have come to speak to you."

Mary said: "Speak on, Holy One. Let me hear the commands of the Lord God."

The Angel said: "I have come with no commands. But since you are specially dear to God, it is permitted that, with my aid, you should look into the future. . . ."

Then Mary looked down at the child and asked eagerly:

"Into *his* future?"

Her face lit up with joyful anticipation.

"Yes," said the Angel gently. "Into *his* future . . . Give me your hand."

Mary stretched out her hand and took that of the Angel. It was like touching flame—yet flame that did not burn. She shrank back a little and the Angel said again:

"Do not be afraid. I am immortal and you are mortal, but my touch shall not hurt you. . . ."

Then the Angel stretched out his great golden wing over the sleeping child and said:

"Look into the future, Mother, and see your Son. . . ."

And Mary looked straight ahead of her and the stable walls melted and dissolved and she was looking into a Garden. It was night and there were stars overhead and a man was kneeling, praying.

Something stirred in Mary's heart, and her motherhood told her that it was her son who knelt there. She said thankfully to herself: "He has become a good man—a devout man—he prays to God." And then suddenly she caught her breath, for the man had raised his face and she saw the agony on it—the despair and the sorrow . . . and she knew that she was looking on greater anguish than any she had ever known or seen. For the man was utterly alone. He was praying to God, praying that this cup of anguish might be taken from him—and there was no answer to his prayer. God was absent and silent. . . .

And Mary cried out:

"Why does not God answer him and give him comfort?"

And she heard the voice of the Angel say:

"It is not God's purpose that he should have comfort."

Then Mary bowed her head meekly and said: "It is not for us to know the inscrutable purposes of God. But has this man—my son—has he no friends? No kindly human friends?"

The Angel rustled his wing and the picture dissolved into another part of the Garden and Mary saw some men lying asleep.

She said bitterly: "He needs them—my son needs them—and they do not care!"

The Angel said: "They are only fallible human creatures. . . ."

Mary murmured to herself: "But he is a *good* man, my son. A good and upright man."

Then again the wing of the Angel rustled, and Mary saw a road winding up a hill, and three men on it carrying crosses, and a crowd behind them and some Roman soldiers.

The Angel said: "What do you see now?"

Mary said: "I see three criminals going to execution."

The left hand man turned his head and Mary saw a cruel crafty face, a low bestial type—and she drew back a little.

"Yes," she said, "they are criminals."

Then the man in the centre stumbled and nearly fell, and

as he turned his face, Mary recognised him and she cried out sharply:

"No, no, it cannot be that my son is a *criminal*!"

But the Angel rustled his wing and she saw the three crosses set up, and the figure hanging in agony on the centre one was the man she knew to be her son. His cracked lips parted and she heard the words that came from them:

"My God, my God, why hast thou forsaken me?"

And Mary cried out: "No, no, it is not true! He cannot have done anything really wrong. There has been some dreadful mistake. It can happen sometimes. There has been some confusion of identity; he has been mistaken for someone else. He is suffering for someone else's crime."

But again the Angel rustled his wings and this time Mary was looking at the figure of the man she revered most on earth—the High Priest of her Church. He was a noble-looking man, and he stood up now and with solemn hands he tore and rent the garment he was wearing, and cried out in a loud voice:

"This man has spoken Blasphemy!"

And Mary looked beyond him and saw the figure of the man who had spoken Blasphemy—and it was her son.

Then the pictures faded and there was only the mudbrick wall of the stable, and Mary was trembling and crying out brokenly:

"I cannot believe it—I *cannot* believe it. We are a God-fearing straight-living family—all my family. Yes, and Joseph's family too. And we shall bring him up carefully to practise religion and to revere and honour the faith of his fathers. A son of ours could never be guilty of blasphemy—I cannot believe it! All this that you have shown me cannot be true."

Then the Angel said: "Look at me, Mary."

And Mary looked at him and saw the radiance surrounding him and the beauty of his Face.

And the Angel said: "What I have shown you is Truth. For I am the Morning Angel, and the Light of the Morning is Truth. Do you believe now?"

And sorely against her will, Mary knew that what she had been shown was indeed Truth . . . and she could not disbelieve any more.

The tears raced down her cheeks and she bent over the child in the manger, her arms outspread as though to protect him. She cried out:

"My child . . . my little helpless child . . . what can I do to save you? To spare you from what is to come? Not only from the sorrow and the pain, but from the evil that will blossom in your heart? Oh indeed it would have been better for you if you had never been born, or if you had died with your first breath. For then you would have gone back to God pure and unsoiled."

And the Angel said: "That is why I have come to you, Mary."

Mary said: "What do you mean?"

The Angel answered: "You have seen the future. It is in your power to say if your child shall live or die."

Then Mary bent her head, and amidst stifled sobs she murmured:

"The Lord gave him to me . . . If the Lord now takes him away, then I see that it may indeed be mercy, and though it tears my flesh I submit to God's will."

But the Angel said softly:

"It is not quite like that. God lays no command on you. The choice is *yours*. You have seen the future. Choose now if the child shall live or die."

Then Mary was silent for a little while. She was a woman who thought slowly. She looked once at the Angel for guidance, but the Angel gave her none. He was golden and beautiful and infinitely remote.

She thought of the pictures that had been shown her—of the agony in the garden, of the shameful death, of a man who, at the hour of death, was forsaken of God, and she heard again the dreadful word *Blasphemy*. . . .

And now, at this moment, the sleeping babe was pure and innocent and happy. . . .

But she did not decide at once, she went on thinking—going over and over again those pictures she had been shown. And in doing so a curious thing happened, for she remembered little things that she had not been aware of seeing at the time. She saw, for instance, the face of the man on the right-hand cross. . . . Not an evil face, only a weak one—and it was turned towards the centre cross and on it was an expression of love and trust and adoration. . . . And it came to Mary, with sudden wonder—"It was at *my son* he was looking like that . . ."

And suddenly, sharply and clearly, she saw her son's face as it had been when he looked down at his sleeping friends in the garden. There was sadness there, and pity and understanding and a great love . . . And she thought: "It is the face of a *good* man . . ." And she saw again the scene of accusation. But this time she looked, not at the splendid High Priest, but at the face of the accused man . . . and in his eyes was no consciousness of guilt. . . .

And Mary's face grew very troubled.

Then the Angel said:

"Have you made your choice, Mary? Will you spare your son suffering and evildoing?"

And Mary said slowly:

"It is not for me, an ignorant and simple woman, to understand the High Purposes of God. The Lord gave me my child. If the Lord takes him away, then that is His will. But since God has given him life, it is not for me to take that life away. For it may be that in my child's life there are things that I do not properly understand . . . It may be that I have seen only *part* of a picture, not the whole. My baby's life is his own, not mine, and I have no right to dispose of it."

"Think again," said the Angel. "Will you not lay your child in my arms and I will bear him back to God?"

"Take him in your arms if it is God's command," said Mary. "But *I* will not lay him there."

There was a great rustling of wings and a blaze of light and the Angel vanished.

Joseph came in a moment later and Mary told him of what had occurred. Joseph approved of what Mary had done.

"You did right, wife," he said. "And who knows, this may have been a lying Angel."

"No," said Mary. "He did not lie."

She was sure of that with every instinct in her.

"I do not believe a word of it all," said Joseph stoutly. "We will bring our son up very carefully and give him good religious instruction, for it is education that counts. He shall work in the shop and go with us to the Synagogue on the Sabbath and keep all the Feasts and the Purifications."

Looking in the manger, he said:

"See, our son is smiling. . . ."

And indeed the boy was smiling and holding out tiny hands to his mother as though to say "Well Done."

But aloft in the vaults of blue, the Angel was quivering with pride and rage.

"To think that I should fail with a foolish, ignorant, woman! Well, there will come another chance. One day when *He* is weary and hungry and weak . . . Then I will take him up to the top of a mountain and show him the Kingdoms of this World of mine. I will offer him the Lordship of them all. He shall control Cities and Kings and Peoples . . . He shall have the Power of causing wars to cease and hunger and oppression to vanish. One gesture of worship to me and he shall be able to establish peace and plenty, contentment and good will—know himself to be a Supreme Power for Good. He can never withstand *that* temptation!"

And Lucifer, Son of the Morning, laughed aloud in ignorance and arrogance and flashed through the sky like a burning streak of fire down to the nethermost depths . . .

In the East, three Watchers of the Heavens came to their Masters and said:

"We have seen a Great Light in the Sky. It must be that some great Personage is born."

But whilst all muttered and exclaimed of Signs and Portents a very old Watcher murmured:

"A Sign from God? God has no need of Signs and Wonders. It is more likely to be a Sign from Satan. It is in my mind that if God were to come amongst us, he would come very quietly. . . ."

But in the Stable there was much fun and good company. The

ass brayed, and the horses neighed and the oxen lowed, and men and women crowded in to see the baby and passed him from one to the other, and he laughed and crowed and smiled at them all.

"See," they cried. "He loves everybody! There never was such a Child. . . ."

A Wreath for Christmas

When Mary made a Holly wreath
The blood ran red—ran red.
Another Mary wove the Thorns
That crowned her Master's head.
But the Mistletoe was far away
Across a Western sea,
And the Mistletoe was wreathed around
A Pagan Apple Tree.

In Glastonbury grew a Thorn,
When Joseph came to trade.
And the Holly Bush was common growth
In every wooded glade.
But the Mistletoe was sacred where
The Sun arose each morn,
And the Mistletoe knew nothing of
The Babe in Bethlehem born.

Saint Patrick sailed the stormy seas
To preach the Cross—and so

He found Eve's Tree—with serpent coiled—
And hung with Mistletoe.
"I bid thee, Serpent, leave this Land,
And open, Plant, thine ears."
He preached the Tale of Christ—and Lo!
The Mistletoe wept tears. . . .

The Holly bush has berries red,
Blood-red upon each bough.
The Thorn it blooms with golden flowers,
And Kissing's fashion now.
What will *you* give to Christ the Lord?
O! Pagan Bough so green?
"The Tears that I have shed for One
Whom I have never seen . . ."

Let Man then give his life for Man,
The blood-red berries say,
And Men have love for fellow men,
Where Gorse flowers bloom so gay.
And the Tears of Man be shed for Man
Where Mistletoe gleams white.
Come, pity, love and sacrifice. . . .
God bless us all this night!

The Naughty Donkey

Once upon a time there was a very naughty little donkey. He *liked* being naughty. When anything was put on his back he kicked it off, and he ran after people trying to bite them. His master couldn't do anything with him, so he sold him to another master, and that master couldn't do anything with him and also sold him, and finally he was sold for a few pence to a dreadful old man who bought old worn-out donkeys and killed them by overwork and ill treatment. But the naughty donkey chased the old man and bit him, and then ran away kicking up his heels. He didn't mean to be caught again so he joined a caravan that was going along the road. "Nobody will know who I belong to in all this crowd," thought the donkey.

These people were all going up to the city of Bethlehem, and when they got there they went into a big *Khan* full of people and animals.

The little donkey slipped into a nice cool stable where there was an ox and a camel. The camel was very haughty, like all camels, because camels think that they alone know the hundredth and secret name of God. He was too proud to speak to the donkey, so the donkey began to boast. He loved boasting.

"I am a very unusual donkey," he said, "I have foresight *and* hindsight."

"What is that?" said the ox.

"Like my forelegs—in front of me—and my hind legs—behind me. Why, my great great, thirty-seventh time great grandmother belonged to the Prophet Balaam, and saw with her own eyes the Angel of the Lord!"

But the ox went on chewing and the camel remained proud.

Then a man and a woman came in, and there was a lot of fuss, but the donkey soon found out that there was nothing to fuss about, only a woman going to have a baby which happens every day. And after the baby was born some shepherds came and made a fuss of the baby—but shepherds are very simple folk.

But then some men in long rich robes came.

"V.I.P.s," hissed the camel.

"What's that?" asked the donkey.

"Very Important People," said the camel, "bringing gifts."

The donkey thought the gifts might be something good to eat, so when it was dark he began nosing around. But the first gift was yellow and hard, with no taste, the second made the donkey sneeze, and when he licked the third, the taste was nasty and bitter.

"What stupid gifts," said the donkey, disappointed. But as he stood there by the Manger, the baby stretched out his little hand and caught hold of the donkey's ear, clutching it tight as very young babies will.

And than a very odd thing happened. The donkey didn't want to be naughty any more. For the first time in his life he wanted to be good. And *he* wanted to give the baby a gift—but he hadn't anything to give. The baby seemed to like his ear, but the ear was part of *him*—and then another strange idea came to him. Perhaps he could give the baby *himself*. . . .

It was not very long after that that Joseph came in with a tall stranger. The stranger was speaking urgently to Joseph, and as the donkey stared at them he could hardly believe his eyes!

The stranger seemed to dissolve and in his place stood an Angel of the Lord, a golden figure with wings. But after a moment the Angel changed back again into a mere man.

"Dear dear, I'm seeing things," said the donkey to himself. "It must be all that fodder I ate."

Joseph spoke to Mary.

"We must take the child and flee. There is no time to be lost." His eye fell on the donkey. "We will take this donkey here, and leave money for his owner whoever he may be. In that way no time will be lost."

So they went out on the road from Bethlehem. But as they

came to a narrow place, the Angel of the Lord appeared with a flaming sword, and the donkey turned aside and began to climb the hillside. Joseph tried to turn him back on to the road, but Mary said:

"Let him be. Remember the Prophet Balaam."

And just as they got to the shelter of some olive trees, the soldiers of King Herod came clattering down the road with drawn swords.

"Just like my great grandmother," said the donkey, very pleased with himself. "I wonder if I have foresight as well."

He blinked his eyes—and he saw a dim picture—a donkey fallen into a pit and a man helping to pull it out. . . . "Why, it's my Master, grown up to be a man," said the donkey. Then he saw another picture . . . the same man, riding on a donkey into a city. . . . "Of course," said the donkey. "He's going to be crowned King!"

But the Crown seemed to be, not Gold, but Thorns (the

donkey loved thorns and thistles—but it seemed the wrong thing for a Crown) and there was a smell he knew and feared—the smell of blood; and there was something on a sponge, bitter like the myrrh he had tasted in the stable. . . .

And the little donkey knew suddenly that he didn't want foresight any more. He just wanted to live for the day, to love his little Master and be loved by him, and to carry Him and his mother safely to Egypt.

Gold, Frankincense and Myrrh

Gold, frankincense and myrrh. . . . As Mary stands
Beside the Cross, those are the words that beat
Upon her brain, and make her clench her hands,
On Calvary, in noonday's burning heat.
Gold, frankincense and myrrh. The Magi kneel
By simple shepherds all agog with joy,
And Angels praising God who doth reveal,
His love for men in Christ, the new born Boy.

Where now the incense? Where the kingly gold?
For Jesus only bitter myrrh and woe.
No kingly figure hangs here—just a son
In pain and dying. . . . How shall Mary know
That with his sigh " 'Tis finished," all is told;
Then—in *that* moment—Christ's reign has begun?

The Water Bus

Mrs. Hargreaves didn't like people.

She tried to, because she was a woman of high principle and a religious woman, and she knew very well that one ought to love one's fellow creatures. But she didn't find it easy—and sometimes she found it downright impossible.

All that she could do was, as you might say, to go through the motions. She sent cheques for a little more than she could afford to reputable charities. She sat on committees for worthy objects, and even attended public meetings for abolishing injustices, which was really more effort than anything else, because, of course, it meant close proximity to human bodies, and she hated to be touched. She was able easily to obey the admonitions posted up in public transport, such as: "Don't travel in the rush hour"; because to go in trains and buses, enveloped tightly in a sweltering crowd of humanity, was definitely her idea of hell on earth.

If children fell down in the street, she always picked them up and bought them sweets or small toys to "make them better." She sent books and flowers to sick people in Hospital.

Her largest subscriptions were to communities of nuns in

Africa, because they and the people to whom they ministered, were so far away that she would never have to come in contact with them, and also because she admired and envied the nuns who actually seemed to *enjoy* the work they did, and because she wished with all her heart that she were like them.

She was willing to be just, kind, fair, and charitable to people, so long as she did not have to see, hear or, touch them.

But she knew very well that that was not enough.

Mrs. Hargreaves was a middle-aged widow with a son and daughter who were both married and lived far away, and she herself lived in a flat in comfortable circumstances in London—and she didn't like people and there didn't seem to be anything she could do about it.

She was standing on this particular morning by her daily woman who was sitting sobbing on a chair in the kitchen and mopping her eyes.

"—never told me nothing, she didn't—not her own Mum! Just goes off to this awful place—and how she heard about it, I don't know—and this wicked woman did things to her, and it went septic—or what ever they call it—and they took her off to Hospital and she's lying there now, *dying* . . . Won't say who the man was—not even now. Terrible it is, my own daughter—such a pretty little girl she used to be, lovely curls. I used to dress her ever so nice. Everybody said she was a lovely little thing. . . ."

She gave a gulp and blew her nose.

Mrs. Hargreaves stood there wanting to be kind, but not really knowing how, because she couldn't really *feel* the right kind of feeling.

She made a soothing sort of noise, and said that she was very very sorry. And was there anything she could do?

Mrs. Chubb paid no attention to this query.

"I s'pose I ought to have looked after her better . . . been at home more in the evenings . . . found out what she was up to and who her friends were—but children don't like you poking your nose into their affairs nowadays—and I wanted to make a bit of extra money, too. Not for myself—I'd been thinking of getting Edie a slap-up gramophone—ever so musical she is—or something nice for the home. I'm not one for spending money on *myself.* . . ."

She broke off for another good blow.

"If there is anything I can do?" repeated Mrs. Hargreaves. She suggested hopefully, "A private room in the Hospital?"

But Mrs. Chubb was not attracted by that idea.

"Very kind of you, Madam, but they look after her very well in the ward. And it's more cheerful for her. She wouldn't like to be cooped away in a room by herself. In the ward, you see, there's always something going on."

Yes, Mrs. Hargreaves saw it all clearly in her mind's eye. Lots of women sitting up in bed, or lying with closed eyes; old women smelling of sickness and old age—the smell of poverty and disease percolating through the clean impersonal odour of disinfectants. Nurses scurrying along, with trays of instruments and trolleys of meals, or washing apparatus, and finally the screens going up round a bed . . . The whole picture made her shiver—but she perceived quite clearly that to Mrs. Chubb's daughter there would be solace and distraction in "the ward" because Mrs. Chubb's daughter liked people.

Mrs. Hargreaves stood there by the sobbing mother and longed for the gift she hadn't got. What she wanted was to be able to put her arm round the weeping woman's shoulder and say something completely fatuous like "There, there, my dear"—and *mean it*. But going through the motions would be no good at all. Actions without feeling were useless. They were without content . . .

Quite suddenly Mrs. Chubb gave her nose a final trumpet-like blow and sat up.

"There," she said brightly. "I feel better.

She straightened a scarf on her shoulders and looked up at Mrs. Hargreaves with a sudden and astonishing cheerfulness.

"Nothing like a good cry, is there?"

Mrs. Hargreaves had never had a good cry. Her griefs had always been inward and dark. She didn't quite know what to say.

"Does you good talking about things," said Mrs. Chubb. "I'd best get on with the washing up. We're nearly out of tea and butter, by the way. I'll have to run round to the shops."

Mrs. Hargreaves said quickly that she would do the washing up and would also do the shopping and she urged Mrs. Chubb to go home in a taxi.

Mrs. Chubb said no point in a taxi when the 11 bus got you there just as quick; so Mrs. Hargreaves gave her two pound notes and said perhaps she would like to take her daughter something in Hospital? Mrs. Chubb thanked her and went.

Mrs. Hargreaves went to the sink and knew that once again she had done the wrong thing. Mrs. Chubb would have much preferred to clink about in the sink, retailing fresh bits of information of a *macabre* character from time to time, and then she could have gone to the shops and met plenty of her fellow kind and talked to *them*, and *they* would have had relatives in hospitals, too, and they all could have exchanged stories. In that way the time until Hospital visiting hours would have passed quickly and pleasantly.

"Why do I always do the wrong thing?" thought Mrs. Hargreaves, washing up deftly and competently; and had no need to search for the answer. *"Because I don't care for people."*

When she had stacked everything away, Mrs. Hargreaves took a shopping bag and went to shop. It was Friday and therefore a busy day. There was a crowd in the butcher's shop. Women pressed against Mrs. Hargreaves, elbowed her aside, pushed baskets and bags between her and the counter. Mrs. Hargreaves always gave way.

"Excuse me, *I* was here before you." A tall thin olive-skinned woman infiltrated herself. It was quite untrue and they both knew it, but Mrs. Hargreaves stood politely back. Unfortunately, she acquired a defender, one of those large brawny women who are public spirited and insist on seeing justice is done.

"You didn't ought to let her push you around, luv," she admonished, leaning heavily on Mrs. Hargreaves' shoulder and breathing gusts of strong peppermint in her face. "You was here long before she was. I come in right on her heels and I know. Go on now." She administered a fierce dig in the ribs. "Push in there and stand up for your rights!"

"It really doesn't matter," said Mrs. Hargreaves. "I'm not in a hurry."

Her attitude pleased nobody.

The original thruster, now in negotiation for a pound and a half of frying steak, turned and gave battle in a whining slightly foreign voice.

"If you think you get here before me, why not you say? No good being so high and mighty and saying" (she mimicked the words) "*it doesn't matter*! How do you think that makes *me* feel? *I* don't want to go out of my turn."

"Oh no," said Mrs. Hargreaves' champion with heavy irony. "Oh no, of course not! We all know that, don't we?"

She looked round and immediately obtained a chorus of assent. The thruster seemed to be well known.

"We know her and her ways," said one woman darkly.

"Pound and a half of rump," said the butcher thrusting forth a parcel. "Now then, come along, who's next, please?"

Mrs. Hargreaves made her purchases and escaped to the street, thinking how really awful people were!

She went into the greengrocer next, to buy lemons and a lettuce. The woman at the greengrocer's was, as usual, affectionate.

"Well, ducks, what can we do for you today?" She rang up the cash register; said "Ta" and "Here you are, dearie," as she pressed a bulging bag into the arms of an elderly gentleman who looked at her in disgust and alarm.

"She always calls me that," the old gentleman confided gloomily when the woman had gone in search of lemons.

" 'Dear,' and 'Dearie' and 'Love.' I don't even know the woman's name!"

Mrs. Hargreaves said she thought it was just a fashion. The old gentleman looked dubious and moved off, leaving Mrs. Hargreaves feeling faintly cheered by the discovery of a fellow sufferer.

Her shopping bag was quite heavy by now, so she thought she would take a bus home. There were three or four people waiting at the bus stop, and an ill-tempered conductress shouted at the passengers.

"Come along now, hurry along, please—we can't wait here all day." She scooped up an elderly arthritic lady and thrust her staggering into the bus where someone caught her and steered her to a seat, and seized Mrs. Hargreaves by the arm above the elbow with iron fingers, causing her acute pain.

"Inside, only. Full up now." She tugged violently at a bell, the bus shot forward and Mrs. Hargreaves collapsed on top of a large woman occupying, through no fault of her own, a good three-quarters of a seat for two.

"I'm so sorry," gasped Mrs. Hargreaves.

"Plenty of room for a little one," said the large woman cheerfully, doing her best without success to make herself smaller. "Nasty temper some of these girls have, haven't they? I prefer the black men myself. Nice and polite *they* are—don't hustle you. Help you in and out quite carefully."

She breathed good temper and onions impartially over Mrs. Hargreaves.

"I don't want any remarks from you, thank you," said the bus conductress who was now collecting fares. "I'd have you know we've got our schedule to keep."

"That's why the bus was idling alongside the curb at the last stop but one," said the large woman. "Fourpenny, please."

Mrs. Hargreaves arrived home exhausted by recrimination and unwanted affection, and also suffering from a bruised arm. The flat seemed peaceful and she sank down gratefully.

Almost immediately however, one of the porters arrived to

clean the windows and followed her round telling her about his wife's mother's gastric ulcer.

Mrs. Hargreaves picked up her handbag and went out again. She wanted—badly—a desert island. Since a desert island was not immediately obtainable (indeed, it would probably entail a visit to a travel agency, a passport office, vaccination, possibly a foreign visa to be obtained, and many other human contacts) she strolled down to the river.

"A water bus," she thought hopefully.

There were such things, she believed. Hadn't she read about them? And there was a pier—a little way along the Embankment; she had seen people coming off it. Of course, perhaps a water bus would be just as crowded as anything else . . .

But here she was in luck. The steamer, or water bus, or whatever it was, was singularly empty. Mrs. Hargreaves bought a ticket to Greenwich. It was the slack time of day and it was not a particularly nice day, the wind being distinctly chilly, so few people were on the water for pleasure.

There were some children in the stern of the boat with a weary adult in charge, and a couple of nondescript men, and an old woman in rusty black. In the bow of the boat there was only a solitary man; so Mrs. Hargreaves went up to the bow, as far from the noisy children as possible.

The boat drew away from the pier out into the Thames. It was peaceful here on the water. Mrs. Hargreaves felt soothed and serene for the first time today. She had got away from—from *what* exactly? "Away from it all!" That was the phrase, but she didn't know exactly what it meant. . . .

She looked gratefully around her. Blessed, blessed water. So—so *insulating*. Boats plied their way up and down stream, but they had nothing to do with *her*. People on land were busy with their own affairs. Let them be—she hoped they enjoyed themselves. Here she was in a boat, being carried down the river towards the sea.

There were stops, people got off, people got on. The boat resumed its course. At the Tower of London the noisy children got off. Mrs. Hargreaves hoped amiably that they would enjoy the Tower of London.

Now they had passed through the Docks. Her feeling of happiness and serenity grew stronger. The eight or nine people still on board were all huddled together in the stern—out of the wind, she supposed. For the first time she paid a little more attention to her fellow traveller in the bows. An Oriental of some kind, she thought vaguely. He was wearing a long capelike coat of some woollen material. An Arab, perhaps? Or a Berber? Not an Indian.

What beautiful material the cloth of his coat was. It seemed to be woven all in one piece. So finely woven, too. She obeyed an almost irresistible impulse to touch it. . . .

• • •

She could never recapture afterwards the feeling that the touch of the coat brought her. It was quite indescribable. It was like what happens when you shake a kaleidoscope. The parts of it are the same parts, but they are arranged differently; they are arranged in a new pattern. . . .

She had wanted when she got on the water bus to escape from herself and the pattern of her morning. She had not escaped in the way she had meant to escape. She was still herself and she was still in the pattern, going through it all over again in her mind. But it was different this time. It was a different pattern because *she* was different.

She was standing again by Mrs. Chubb—poor Mrs. Chubb— She heard the story again only this time it was a different story. It was not so much what Mrs. Chubb said, but what she had been feeling—her despair and—yes, her guilt. Because, of course, she was secretly blaming herself, striving to tell herself how she had done everything for her girl—her lovely little girl—recalling the frocks she had bought her and the sweets—and how she had given in to her when she wanted things—she had gone out to work, too—but of course, in her innermost mind, Mrs. Chubb knew that it was not a gramophone for Edie she had been working for, but a washing machine—a washing machine like Mrs. Peters had down the road (and so stuck up about it, too!). It was her own fierce housepride that had set her fingers to toil. True, she had given Edie things all her life—plenty of them—but had she *thought* about Edie enough? Thought about the boyfriends she was making? Thought about asking her friends to the house—seeing if there wasn't some kind of party at home Edie could have? Thinking about Edie's character, her life, what would be best for her? Trying to find out more about Edie because after all, Edie was *her* business—the real paramount business of her life. And she mustn't be stupid about it! Good will wasn't enough. One had to manage not to be stupid, too.

In fancy, Mrs. Hargreaves' arm went round Mrs. Chubb's shoulder. She thought with affection: "You poor stupid dear. It's not as bad as you think. *I* don't believe she's dying at all." Of course Mrs. Chubb had exaggerated, had sought deliberately for tragedy, because that was the way Mrs. Chubb saw life—in melodramatic terms. It made life less drab, easier to live. Mrs. Hargreaves understood so well. . . .

Other people came into Mrs. Hargreaves' mind. Those women enjoying their fight at the butcher's counter. Characters, all of them. Fun, really! Especially the big red-faced woman with her passion for justice. She really liked a good row!

Why on earth, Mrs. Hargreaves wondered, had she minded the woman at the greengrocer's calling her "Luv"? It was a kindly term.

That bad-tempered bus conductress—why—her mind probed, came up with a solution. Her young man had stood her up the evening before. And so she hated everybody, hated her monotonous life, wanted to make other people feel her power—one could so easily feel like that if things went wrong. . . .

The kaleidoscope shook—changed. She was no longer *looking* at it—she was inside it—*part of it*. . . .

The boat hooted. She sighed, moved, opened her eyes. They had come at last to Greenwich.

• • •

Mrs. Hargreaves went back by train from Greenwich. The train, at this time of day, the lunch hour, was almost empty.

But Mrs. Hargreaves wouldn't have cared if it had been full. . . .

Because, for a brief space of time, she was at one with her fellow beings. *She liked people.* Almost—she loved them!

It wouldn't last, of course. She knew that. A complete change of character was not within the bounds of reality. But she was deeply, humbly, and comprehendingly grateful for what she had been given.

She knew now what the thing that she had coveted was like. She knew the warmth of it, and the happiness—knew it, not from intelligent observation from without, but from within. From *feeling* it.

And perhaps, knowing now just what it was, she could learn the beginning of the road to it. . . ?

She thought of the coat woven in the harmony of one piece. She had not been able to see the man's face. But she thought she knew who He was. . . .

Already the warmth and the vision were fading. But she would not forget—she would never forget!

"Thank you," said Mrs. Hargreaves, speaking from the depths of a grateful heart.

She said it aloud in the empty railway carriage.

The mate of the water bus was staring at the tickets in his hand.

"Where's t'other one?" he asked.

"Whatchermean?" said the Captain who was preparing to go ashore for lunch.

"Must be someone on board still. Eight passengers there was. I counted them. And I've only got seven tickets here."

"Nobody left on board. Look for yourself. One of 'em must have got off without your noticing 'im—either that or he walked on the water!"

And the Captain laughed heartily at his own joke.

In the Cool of the Evening

The church was fairly full. Evensong, nowadays, was always better attended than morning service.

Mrs. Grierson and her husband knelt side by side in the fifth pew on the pulpit side. Mrs. Grierson knelt decorously, her elegant back curved. A conventional worshipper, one would have said, breathing a mild and temperate prayer.

But there was nothing mild about Janet Grierson's petition. It sped upwards into space on wings of fire.

"God, help him! Have mercy upon him. Have mercy upon *me*. Cure him, Lord. Thou hast all power. Have mercy—have mercy. Stretch out Thy hand. Open his mind. He's such a sweet boy—so gentle—so innocent. Let him be healed. Let him be *normal*. Hear me, Lord. Hear me . . . Ask of me anything you like, but stretch out Thy hand and make him whole. Oh God, *hear* me. *Hear* me. With Thee all things are possible. My faith shall make him whole—I *have* faith—I believe. I *believe*! Help me!"

The people stood. Mrs. Grierson stood with them. Elegant, fashionable, composed. The service proceeded.

The Rector mounted the steps of the pulpit, gave out his text.

Part of the 95th psalm; the tenth verse. Part of the psalm we sing every Sunday morning. "It is a people who do err in their hearts, for they have not known my ways."

The Rector was a good man, but not an eloquent one. He strove to give to his listeners the thought that the words had conveyed to him. A people that erred, not in what they *did*, not in *actions* displeasing to God, not in overt sin—but a people not even knowing that they erred. A people who, quite simply, did not know God . . . They did not know what God was, what he wanted, how he showed himself. They could know. That was the point the Rector was striving to make. Ignorance is no defence. They *could* know.

He turned to the East.

"And now to God the Father. . . ."

He'd put it very badly, the Rector thought sadly. He hadn't made his meaning clear at all. . . .

Quite a good congregation this evening. How many of them, he wondered, really *knew* God?

Again Janet Grierson knelt and prayed with fervour and desperation. It was a matter of will, of concentration. If she could get through—God was all powerful. If she could reach him. . . .

For a moment she felt she was getting there—and then there was the irritating rustle of people rising; sighs, movements. Her husband touched her arm. Unwillingly she rose. Her face was very pale. Her husband looked at her with a slight frown. He was a quiet man who disliked intensity of any kind.

In the porch friends met them.

"What an attractive hat, Janet. It's new, isn't it?"

"Oh no, it's terribly old."

"Hats are so difficult," Mrs. Stewart complained. "One hardly ever wears one in the country and then on Sunday one feels odd. Janet, do you know Mrs. Lamphrey—Mrs. Grierson. Major Grierson. The Lamphreys have taken Island Lodge."

"I'm so glad," said Janet, shaking hands. "It's a delightful house."

"Everyone says we'll be flooded out in winter," said Mrs. Lamphrey ruefully.

"Oh no—not *most* years."

"But *some* years? I knew it! But the children were mad about it. And of course they'd adore a flood."

"How many have you?"

"Two boys and a girl."

"Edward is just the same age as our Johnnie," said Mrs. Stewart. "I suppose he'll be going to his public school next year. Johnnie's going to Winchester."

"Oh, Edward is much too much of a moron ever to pass

common entrance, I'm sure," sighed Mrs. Lamphrey. "He doesn't care for anything but games. We'll have to send him to a cram-mer's. Isn't it terrible, Mrs. Grierson, when one's children turn out to be morons?"

Almost at once, she felt the chill. A quick change of subject—the forthcoming fête at Wellsly Park.

As the groups moved off in varying directions, Mrs. Stewart said to her friend:

"Darling, I ought to have warned you!"

"Did I say something wrong? I thought so—but what?"

"The Griersons. Their boy. They've only got one. And *he's* subnormal. Mentally retarded."

"Oh how awful—but I couldn't know. Why does one always go and put one's foot straight into things?"

"It's just that Janet's rather sensitive. . . ."

As they walked along the field path, Rodney Grierson said gently,

"They didn't mean anything. That woman didn't know."

"No. No, of course she didn't."

"Janet, can't you try—"

"Try what?"

"Try not to mind so much. Can't you accept—"

Her voice interrupted him, it was high and strained.

"No, I can't *accept*—as you put it. There must be *something* that could be done! He's physically so perfect. It must be just some gland—some perfectly simple thing. Doctors will find out some day. There must be something—injections—hypnotism."

"You only torture yourself, Janet. All these doctors you drag him round to. It worries the boy."

"I'm not like you, Rodney. I don't give up. I prayed *again* in church just now."

"You pray too much."

"How can one pray "too much"? I believe in God, I tell you. I *believe* in him. I have faith—and faith can move mountains."

"You can't give God orders, Janet."

"What an extraordinary thing to say!"

"Well—" Major Grierson shifted uncomfortably.

"I don't think you know what faith is."

"It ought to be the same as trust."

Janet Grierson was not listening.

"Today—in church, I had a terrible feeling. I felt that God wasn't there. I didn't feel that there was no God—just that He was somewhere else . . . But where?"

"Really, Janet!"

"Where could He be? Where could I find Him?"

She calmed herself with an effort as they turned in at the gate of their own house. A stocky middle-aged woman came out smiling to meet them.

"Have a nice service? Supper's almost ready. Ten minutes?"

"Oh good. Thank you, Gertrude. Where's Alan?"

"He's out in the garden as usual. I'll call him."

She cupped her mouth with her hands.

"A—lan. A—lan."

Suddenly, with a rush, a boy came running. He was fair and blue-eyed. He looked excited and happy.

"Daddy—Mummy—look what I've found."

He parted his cupped hands carefully, showing the small creature they contained.

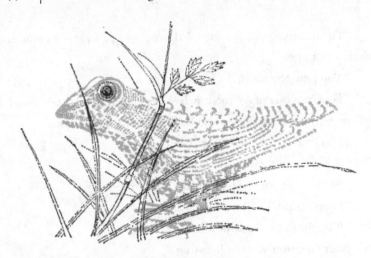

"Ugh, horrible." Janet Grierson turned away with a shudder.

"Don't you like him? Daddy!" He turned to his father. "See, he's partly like a frog—but he isn't a frog—he's got feathers and a sort of wings. He's quite new—not like any other animal."

He came nearer, and dropped his voice.

"I've got a name for him. I call him Raphion. Do you think it's a nice name?"

"Very nice, my boy," said his father with a slight effort.

The boy put the strange creature down.

"Hop away, Raphion, or fly if you can. There he goes. He isn't afraid of me."

"Come and get ready for supper, Alan," said his mother.

"Oh yes, I'm hungry."

"What have you been doing?"

"Oh, I've been down at the end of the garden, talking to a friend. He helps me name the animals. We have such fun."

"He's happy, Janet," said Grierson as the boy ran up the stairs.

"I know. But what's going to become of him? And those horrible things he finds. They're all about everywhere nowadays since the accident at the Research station."

"They'll die out, dear. Mutations usually do."

"Queer heads—and extra legs!" She shuddered.

"Well, think of all the legs centipedes have. You don't mind them?"

"They're natural."

"Perhaps everything has to have a first time."

Alan came running down the stairs again.

"Have you had a nice time? Where did you go? To church?" He laughed, trying the word out. "Church—church—that's a funny name."

"It means God's house," said his mother.

"Does it? I didn't know God lived in a house."

"God is in Heaven, dear. Up in the sky. I told you."

"But not always? Doesn't He come down and walk about? In the evenings? In summer? When it's nice and cool?"

"In the Garden of Eden," said Grierson, smiling.

"No, in this garden, here. He'd like all the funny new animals and things like I do."

Janet winced.

"Those funny animals—darling." She paused. "There was an accident, you know. At the big Station up on the downs. That's why there are so many of these queer—things about. They get born like that. It's very sad!"

"Why? I think it's exciting! Lots of new kinds of things being born all the time. I have to find names for them. Sometimes I think of lovely names."

He wriggled off his chair.

"I've finished. Please—can I go now? My friend is waiting for me in the garden."

His father nodded. Gertrude said softly.

"All children are the same. They always invent a 'friend' to play with."

"At five, perhaps. Not when they're thirteen," said Janet bitterly.

"Try not to mind, dear," said Gertrude gently.

"How can I help it?"

"You may be looking at it all the wrong way."

Down at the bottom of the garden, where it was cool under the trees, Alan found his friend waiting.

He was stroking a rabbit who was not quite a rabbit but something rather different.

"Do you like him, Alan?"

"Oh yes. What shall we call him?"

"It's for you to say."

"Is it really? I shall call him—I shall call him—Forteor. Is that a good name?"

"All your names are good names."

"Have you got a name yourself?"

"I have a great many names."

"Is one of them God?"

"Yes."

"I thought it was! You don't really live in that stone house in the village with the long thing sticking up, do you?"

"I live in many places . . . But sometimes, in the cool of the evening, I walk in a garden—with a friend and talk about the New World—"

Jenny by the Sky

Come down to me, Jenny, come down from the hill
Come down to me here where I wait
Come down to my arms, to my lips, my desire
Come down all my hunger to sate

But Jenny walks lonely, her head in the air,
She walks on the hill top, the wind in her hair,
She will not come down to me, loud though I cry
She walks with the wind, upturned face to the sky . . .

    In the cool of the evening I walked in the glade,
    And there I met God . . . and I was not afraid.
    Together we walked in the depths of the wood
    And together we looked at the things we had made
    Together we looked—and we saw they were good . . .

    God made the World and the stars set on high
    The Galaxies rushing, none knows where or why.
    God fashioned the Cosmos, the Universe wide,

And the hills and the valleys, the birds in the wood
God made them and loved them, and saw they were good . . .

And I—have made Jenny! To walk on the hill.
She will not come down to me loud though I cry;
She walks there for ever, her face to the sky,
She will not come down though I call her,
She will not come down to my greed,
She is as I dreamed her . . . and made her
Of my loving and longing and need . . .

With my mind and my heart I made Jenny,
I made her of love and desire,
I made her to walk on the hill top
In loneliness, beauty and fire. . . .

In the cool of the evening I walked in the wood
And God walked beside me. . . .
                    We both understood.

Promotion in the Highest

They were walking down the hill from the little stone church on the hillside.

It was very early in the morning, the hour just before dawn. There was no one about to see them as they went through the village, though one or two sleepers sighed and stirred in their sleep. The only human being who saw them that morning was Jacob Narracott, as he grunted and sat up in the ditch. He had collapsed there soon after he came out of the Bel and Dragon last night.

He sat up and rubbed his eyes, not quite believing what he saw. He staggered to his feet and shambled off in the direction of his cottage, made uneasy by the trick his eyes had played him. At the crossroads he met George Palk, the village constable, on his beat.

"You'm late getting home, Jacob. Or should I say early?" Palk grinned.

Jacob groaned, and rocked his head in his hands.

"Government's been and done something to the beer," he affirmed. "Meddling again. I never used to feel like this."

"What'll your Missus say when she sees you rolling home at this hour?"

"Won't say anything. She's away to her sister's."

"So you took the opportunity to see the New Year in?"

Jacob grunted. Then he said uneasily: "You seen a lot of people just now, George? Coming along the road?"

"No. What sort of people?"

"Funny people. Dressed odd."

"You mean Beats?"

"Nah, not Beats. Sort of old-fashioned like. Carrying things, some of 'em was."

"What sort of things?"

"Ruddy great wheel, one had—a woman. And there was a man with a gridiron. And one rather nice looking wench, dressed very rich and fancy with a great big basket of roses."

"Roses? This time of year? Was it a sort of procession?"

"That's right. Lights on their heads they had, too."

"Aw, get on, Jacob! Seeing things—that's what's the matter with you. Get on home, put your head under the tap, and sleep it off."

"Funny thing is, I feel I've seen 'em before somewhere—but for the life of me I can't think where."

"Ban the bomb marchers, maybe."

"I tell you they was dressed all rich and funny. Fourteen of them there was. I counted. Walking in pairs mostly."

"Oh well, some New Year's Eve party coming home maybe: but if you ask me, I'd say you did yourself too well at the Bel and Dragon, and that accounts for it all."

"Saw the New Year in proper, we did," agreed Jacob. "Had to celebrate special, seeing as it wasn't only 'Out with the Old Year, and in with the New.' It's out with the old Century and in with the New one. January 1st, A.D. 2000, that's what today is."

"Ought to mean something," said Constable Palk.

"More compulsory evacuation, I suppose," grumbled Jacob. "A man's home's not his castle nowadays. It's out with him, and off to one of these ruddy new towns. Or bundle him off to New Zealand or Australia. Can't even have children now unless the Government says you may. Can't even dump things in your back garden without the ruddy Council coming round and saying its got to go to the village dump. What do they think a back garden's *for*? What it's come to is, nobody treats you like you were *human* any more. . . ."

His voice rumbled away . . .

"Happy New Year," Constable Palk called after him. . . .

The Fourteen proceeded on their way.

St. Catherine was trundling her Wheel in a disconsolate manner. She turned her head and spoke to St. Lawrence who was examining his Gridiron.

"What can I *do* with this thing?" she asked.

"I suppose a wheel always comes in useful," said St. Lawrence doubtfully.

"What for?"

"I see what you mean—it was meant for torture—for breaking a man's body."

"Broken on the wheel." St. Catherine gave a little shudder. "What are you going to do with your gridiron?"

"I thought perhaps I might use it for cooking something."

"Pfui," said St. Cristina as they passed a dead stoat.

St. Elizabeth of Hungary handed her one of her roses.

St. Cristina sniffed it gratefully. St. Elizabeth fell back beside St. Peter.

"I wonder why we all seem to have paired up," she said thoughtfully.

"Those do, perhaps, who have something in common," suggested Peter.

"Have we something in common?"

"Well, we're both of us liars," said Peter cheerfully.

In spite of a lie that would never be forgotten, Peter was a very honest man. He accepted the truth of himself.

"I know. I know!" Elizabeth cried. "I can't bear to remember. How could I have been so cowardly—so weak, that day? Why didn't I stand there bravely and say, "I am taking bread to the hungry?" Instead, my husband shouts at me, "What have you got in that basket?" And I shiver and stammer out "Nothing but roses . . ." And he snatched off the cover of the basket"—"And it *was* roses," said Peter gently.

"Yes. A miracle happened. Why did my Master do that for me? Why did he acquiesce in my lie? Why? Oh why?"

St. Peter looked at her.

He said:

"So that you should never forget. So that pride could never lay hold of you. So that you should know that you were weak and not strong."

"I, too—" He stopped and then went on.

"I who was so sure that I could never deny him, so certain that I, above all the others, would be steadfast. I was the one who denied and spoke those lying cowardly words. Why did he choose *me*—a man like me? He founded his Church on me—Why?"

"That's easy," said Elizabeth. "Because you loved him. I think you loved him more than any of the others did."

"Yes, I loved him. I was one of the first to follow him. There was I, mending the nets, and I looked up, and there he was watching me. And he said, 'Come with me.' And I went. I think I loved him from the very first moment."

"You are so nice, Peter," said Elizabeth.

St. Peter swung his keys doubtfully.

"I'm not sure about that Church I founded . . . It's not turned out at all as we meant. . . ."

"Things never do. You know," Elizabeth went on thoughtfully. "I'm sorry now I put that leper in my husband's bed. It seemed at the time a fine defiant Act of Faith. But really—well, it wasn't very *kind*, was it?"

St. Appolonia stopped suddenly in her tracks.

"I'm so sorry," she said. "I've dropped my tooth. That's the worst of having such a small emblem."

She called: "Anthony. Come and find it for me."

They were in the Land of the Saints now, and as they breathed its special fragrance St. Cristina cried aloud in joy. The Holy Birds sang, and the Harps played.

But the Fourteen did not linger. They pressed forward to the Court of Assembly.

The Archangel Gabriel received them.

"The Court is in Session," he said. "Enter."

The Assembly Chamber was wide and lofty. The walls were made of mist and cloud.

The Recording Angel was writing in his Golden Book. He laid it aside, opened his Ledger and said, "Names and addresses, please."

They told him their names and gave their address. St. Petrock-on-the-Hill. Stickle Buckland.

"Present your Petition," said the Recording Angel.

St. Peter stepped forward.

"There is unrest amongst us. We ask to go back to Earth."

"Isn't Heaven good enough for you?" asked the Recording Angel. There was, perhaps, a slight tinge of sarcasm in his voice.

"It is too good for us."

The Recording Angel adjusted his Golden Wig, put on his Golden Spectacles, and looked over the top of them with disapprobation.

"Are you questioning the decision of your Creator?"

"We would not dare—but there was a ruling—"

The Archangel Gabriel, as Mediator and Intermediary between Heaven and Earth, rose.

"If I may submit a point of law?"

The Recording Angel inclined his head.

"It was laid down, by Divine decree, that in the Year A.D. 1000 and in every subsequent 1000th Year, there should be fresh Judgments and Decisions on such points as were brought to a special Court of Appeal. Today is the Second Millennium. I submit that every person who has ever lived on earth has today a right of Appeal."

The Recording Angel opened a large Gold Tome and consulted it. Closing it again, he said:

"Set out your Case."

St. Peter spoke.

"We died for our Faith. Died joyfully. We were rewarded. Rewarded far beyond our deserts. We—he hesitated and turned to a young man with a beautiful face and burning eyes. "You explain."

"It was not enough," said the young man.

"Your reward was not enough?" The Recording Angel looked scandalised.

"Not our reward. Our service. To die for the Faith, to be a Saint, is not enough to merit Eternal Life. You know my story. I was rich. I obeyed the Law. I kept the commandments. It was not enough. I went to the Master. I said to him: "Master, what shall I do to inherit Eternal Life?""

"You were told what to do, and you did it," said the Recording Angel.

"It was not enough."

"You did more. After you had given all your possessions to the poor, you joined the disciples in their mission. You suffered Martyrdom. You were stoned to death in Ephesus."

"It was not enough."

"What more do you want to do?"

"We had Faith—burning Faith. We had the Faith that can move mountains. Two thousand years have taught us that we could have done more. We did not always have enough Compassion. . . ."

The word came from his lips like a breath from a summer sea. It whispered all round the Heavens. . . .

"This is our petition: Let us go back to Earth in Pity and Compassion to help those who need help."

There was a murmur of agreement from those around him.

The Recording Angel picked up the Golden Intercom on his desk. He spoke into it in a low murmur.

He listened. . . .

Then he spoke—briskly, and with authority.

"Promotion Granted," he said. "Approval in the Highest."

They turned to go, their faces radiant.

"Hand in your Crowns and Halos at the door, please."

They surrendered their Crowns and Halos and went out of the Court. St. Thomas came back.

"Excuse me," he said politely. "But what you said just now—was it *Permission* Granted? Or was it *Promotion* Granted?"

"Promotion. After two thousand years of Sainthood, you are moving up to a higher rank."

"Thank you. I *thought* it was promotion you said. But I wanted to make *sure*."

He followed the others.

"He always had to make sure," said Gabriel. "You know—sometimes—I can't help wondering what it would be like to have an immortal soul. . . ."

The Recording Angel looked horrified.

"Do be careful, Gabriel. You know what happened to Lucifer."

"Sometimes I can't help feeling a little sorry for Lucifer. Having to rank below Adam upset him terribly. Adam wasn't much, was he?"

"A poor type," agreed the Recording Angel. "But he and all his descendants were created in the image of God with immortal souls. They *have* to rank above the Angels."

"I've often thought Adam's soul must have been a very small one."

"There has to be a beginning for everything," the Recording Angel pointed out severely.

Mrs. Badstock heaved and pulled. The smell of the village dump was not agreeable. It was an unsightly mass of old tyres, broken chairs, ragged quilts, old kerosene tins, and broken bedsteads. All the things that nobody could possibly want. But Mrs. Badstock was tugging hopefully. If that old pram was anyway repairable—She heaved again and it came free. . . .

"Drat!" said Mrs. Badstock. The upper portion of the pram was not too bad, but the wheels were missing.

She threw it down angrily.

"Can I help you?" A woman spoke out of the darkness.

"No good. Blasted thing's got no wheels."

"You want a wheel? I've got one here."

"Ta, ducks. But I need four. And anyway, yours is much too big."

"That's why I thought we could make it into four—with a little adjustment." The woman's fingers strayed over it pushing, pulling.

"There! How's that?"

"Well, I never! However did you—Now, if we'd got a nail or two—or a screw. I'll get my hubby—"

"I think I can manage." She bent over the pram. Mrs. Badstock peered down to try and see what was happening.

The other woman straightened up suddenly. The pram stood on four wheels.

"It will want a little oil, and some new lining."

"I can see to that easy! *What* a boon it will be. You're quite a little home mechanic, aren't you, ducks? How on earth did you manage it?"

"I don't know really," said St. Catherine vaguely. "It just—happens."

The tall woman in the brocade dress said with authority: "Bring them up to the house. There's plenty of room."

The man and the woman looked at her suspiciously. Their six children did the same.

"The Council are finding us somewhere," said the man sullenly.

"But they're going to separate us," said the woman.

"And you don't want that?"

"Of course we don't."

Three of the children began to cry.

"Shut your bloody mouths," said the man, but without rancour.

"Been saying they'd evict us for a long time," said the man. "Now they've done it. Always whining about their rent. I've better things to do with my money than pay rent. That's Councils all over for you."

He was not a nice man. His wife was not very nice either, St. Barbara thought. But they loved their children.

"You'd better all come up to my place," she said.

"Where is it?"

"Up there." She pointed.

They turned to look.

"But—that's a *Castle*," the woman exclaimed in awestruck tones.

"Yes, it's a Castle all right. So you see, there will be lots of room. . . ."

• • •

St. Scoithín stood rather doubtfully on the seashore. He wasn't quite sure what to do with his Salmon.

He could smoke it, of course—it would last longer that way. The trouble was that it was really only the rich who like smoked salmon, and the rich had quite enough things already. The poor much preferred their salmon in tins. Perhaps—

The Salmon writhed in his hands, and St. Scoithín jumped.

"Master," said the Salmon.

St. Scoithín looked at it.

"It is nearly a thousand years since I saw the sea," said the Salmon pleadingly.

St. Scoithín smiled at him affectionately. He walked out on the sea, and lowered the Salmon gently into the water.

"Go with God," he said.

He walked back to the shore, and almost immediately stumbled over a big heap of tins of salmon with a purple flower stuck on top of them.

St. Cristina was walking along a crowded City street. The traffic roared past her. The air was full of diesel fumes.

"This is terrible," said St. Cristina, holding her nose. "I must do something about this. And why don't they empty the dustbins oftener? It's very bad for people." She pondered. "Perhaps I had better go into Parliament. . . ."

St. Peter was busy setting out his Loaf and Fish stall.

"Old Age Pensioners first," he said. "Come on, Granddad."

"Are you National Assistance?" the old man asked suspiciously.

"That kind of thing."

"Not religious, is it? I'm not going to sing hymns."

"When the food's all gone, I shall preach," said Peter. "But you don't have to stay on and listen."

"Sounds fair enough. What are you going to preach about?"

"Something quite simple. Just how to attain Eternal Life."

A younger man gave a hoot of laughter.

"Eternal Life! What a hope!"

"Yes," said Peter cheerfully, as he shovelled out parcels of hot fish. "It *is* a hope. Got to remember that. There's always Hope."

In the Church of St. Petrock-on-the-Hill, the Vicar was sitting sadly in a pew, watching a confident young architect examining the old painted screen.

"Sorry, Vicar," said the young man, turning briskly. "Not a hope in Hell, I'm afraid. Oh! sorry again. I oughtn't to have put it like that. But it's long past restoring. Nothing to be done. The wood's rotten, and there's hardly any paint left—not enough to see what the original was like. What is it? Fifteenth century?"

"Late fourteenth."

"What are they? Saints?"

"Yes. Seven each side." He recited. "St. Lawrence, St. Thomas, St. Andrew, St. Anthony, St. Peter, St. Scoithín, and one we don't know. The other side: St. Barbara, St. Catherine, St. Appolonia, St. Elizabeth of Hungary, St. Cristina the Astonishing, St. Margaret, and St. Martha."

"You've got it all very pat."

"There were church records. Not in very good condition. Some we had to make out by their emblems—St. Barbara's castle for instance, and St. Lawrence's gridiron. The original work was done by Brother Bernard of the Benedictines of Froyle Abbey."

"Well, I'm sorry about my verdict. But everything has got to go sometime. I hear your rich parishioner has offered you a new screen with modern symbolical figures on it?"

"Yes," said the Vicar without enthusiasm.

"Seen the big new Cathedral Centre at New Huddersfield? Coventry was good in its time, but this is streets ahead of it! Takes a bit of getting used to, of course."

"I am sure it would."

"But it's taken on in a big way! Modern. Those old Saints," he flicked a hand towards the screen. "I don't suppose anyone knows who half of them are nowadays. I certainly don't. Who was St. Cristina the Astonishing?"

"Quite an interesting character. She had a very keen sense of smell. At her funeral service the smell of her putrefying body affected her so much that she levitated out of her coffin up to the roof of the Chapel."

"Whew! Some Saint! Oh well, it takes all sorts to make a world. Even your old Saints would be very different nowadays, I expect. . . ."

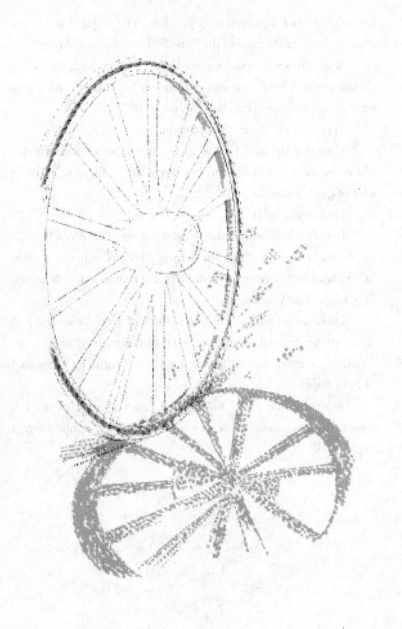

The Saints of God

Saint Lawrence with his Gridiron
Saint Catherine with her Wheel
Saint Margaret with her Dragon
Saint Wilfred with his Seal

The Saints of God are marching
Are marching down the hill
The Saints of God are marching
To ascertain God's Will

"Oh, we have sat in Glory
And worn the Martyr's Crown
But we now make petition
That we from Heaven go down.

"In pity and compassion
Let us go back to men
And show them where the Pathway
Leads back to Heaven again. . . ."

The Island

There were hardly any trees on the island. It was arid land, an island of rock, and the goats could find little to eat. The shapes of the rocks were beautiful as they swept up from the sea, and their colour changed with the changing of the light, going from rose to apricot, to pale misty grey, deepening to mauve and to stern purple, and in a last fierceness to orange, as the sun sank into that sea so rightly called wine-dark. In the early mornings the sky was a pale proud blue, and seemed so high up and so far away that it filled one with awe to look up at it.

But the women of the island did not look up at it often, unless they were anxiously gazing for signs of a storm. They were women and they had to work. Since food was scarce, they worked hard and unceasingly, so that they and their children should live. The men went out daily in the fishing boats. The children herded the goats and played little games of their own with pebbles in the sun.

Today the women with great jars of fresh water on their heads, toiled up the slope from the spring in the cleft of the cliff, to the village above.

Mary was still strong, but she was not as young as most of the women, and it was an effort to her to keep pace with them.

Today the women were very gay, for in a few days' time there was to be a wedding. The girl children danced round their elders and chanted monotonously:

"I shall go to the wedding . . . I shall go to the wedding . . . I shall have a ribbon in my hair . . . I shall eat roseleaf jelly . . . roseleaf jelly in a spoon. . . ."

The mothers laughed, and one child's mother said teasingly: "How do you know I shall take you to the wedding?"

Dismayed, the child stared.

"You *will* take me—you will—you *will*. . . ." And she clung to Mary, demanding: "She will let me go to the wedding? Say she will!"

And Mary smiled and said gently: "I think she will, sweetheart!"

And all the women laughed gaily, for today they were all happy and excited because of the wedding.

"Have you ever been to a wedding, Mary?" the child asked.

"She went to her own," laughed one of the women.

"I didn't mean your own. I meant a wedding party, with dancing and sweet things to eat, and roseleaf jam, and honey?"

"Yes. I have been to weddings." Mary smiled, "I remember one wedding . . . very well . . . a long time ago."

"With roseleaf jam?"

"I think so—yes. And there was wine. . . ."

Her voice trailed off as she remembered.

"And when the wine runs out, we have to drink water," one of the women said. "That always happens!"

"We did not drink water at this wedding!"

Mary's voice was strong and proud.

The other women looked at her. They knew that Mary had come here with her son from a long way away, and that she did not often speak of her life in earlier days, and that there was some very good reason for that. They were careful not to ask her questions, but of course there were rumours, and now suddenly one of the older children piped up and spoke like a parrot.

"They say you had a son who was a great criminal and was executed for his crimes. Is that true?"

The women tried to hush her down, but Mary spoke, her eyes looking straight ahead of her.

"Those that should know said he was a criminal."

"But you didn't think so?" the child persisted.

Mary said after a pause:

"I do not know of myself what is right or wrong. I am too ignorant. My son loved people—good and bad equally. . . ."

They had reached the village now and they divided to go to their own homes. Mary had farthest to go, to a stone croft at the very end of the cluster of sprawling buildings.

"How is your son? Well, I hope?" asked one of the women politely.

"He is well, thanks be to God."

To erase the memory of what had been said before, the woman said kindly:

"You must be proud of this son of yours. We all know that he is a Holy Man. They say he has visions and walks with God."

"He is a good son," said Mary. "And, as you say, a very Holy Man."

She left them to go her own way and they stood looking after her for a moment or two.

"She is a good woman."

"Yes. It is not her fault, I am sure, that her other son went wrong."

"Such things happen. One does not know why. But she is lucky in this son. There are times when he is animated by the Spirit, and then he prophesies in a loud voice. His feet, they say, rise off the ground—and then he lies like one dead for a while."

They all nodded and clucked in wonder and pleasure to have such a holy man amongst them.

Mary went to the little stone cottage, and stood the jar of water down. She glanced towards where a man sat at a rudely fashioned table. There was a scroll of parchment in front of him and he bent over it, writing with a pen, pausing now and then, whilst his eyes half closed, as he lost himself in the ardours of the spirit. . . .

Mary was careful not to disturb him. She busied herself in getting together the midday meal.

The man was a man of great beauty, though no longer young. He had great delicacy of feature, and the far-away eyes of a soul to whom spiritual life is as real as the life of the body. Presently his hand slackened on the pen, and he seemed almost to pass into a trance, neither moving nor speaking, and indeed hardly breathing.

Mary put the dishes on the table.

"Your meal is ready, my son."

As one who hears a faint sound from very far away, he shook his head impatiently.

"The vision . . . so near . . ." he muttered, "so near . . . When—oh when?"

"Come, my son, eat."

He waved the food away.

"There is another hunger, another thirst! The food of the spirit
. . . The thirst for righteousness. . . ."

"But you must eat. To please me. To please your mother."

Gently she coaxed and scolded—and at last he came down
from that high exaltation, and smiled at her with a human half-
teasing look.

"Must I then eat to satisfy you?"

"Yes. Or else I shall be made unhappy."

So he ate to please her, hardly noticing what the food was.

Then he bethought himself to ask:

"How is it with you, dear mother? You have all you need?"

"I have all I need," said Mary.

He nodded, satisfied, and took up his pen once more.

When Mary had cleared all away, she went out and stood look-
ing out over the sea.

Her hands clasped together, she bowed her head and spoke
softly under her breath.

"Have I done all I could? I am such an ignorant woman. I do
not always know how to serve and minister to one who is assuredly
a Saint of God. I wash his linen, and prepare his food, and bring
him fresh water, and wash his feet. But more than that I know not
how to do."

As she stood there, her anxiety passed. Serenity came back to
her worn face.

On the shore beneath, a boat had drawn into the little stone
pier. It was not an ordinary fishing boat, but one that stood high in
the water, and had a big curving prow of richly carved wood. Two

men landed from it, and some old men who were mending fishing nets came to accost the strangers.

Politely the two men made known their business.

"We seek amongst the islands hereabouts for an island on which is said to dwell the Queen of Heaven."

The old fishermen shook their heads.

"What you seek is certainly not here. We have no shrine such as you describe."

"Perhaps your women have knowledge of such a shrine?" one of the strangers suggested. "Women are often secretive about such matters."

"Inquire if you wish. One of us will go up and show you the village."

The strangers went up with their guide. The women came clustering out of their houses. They were excited and interested, but they all shook their heads.

"No Goddess has her Shrine here, alas! Neither by our Spring nor elsewhere."

They told him of other shrines reported from other places, but none of them were what the strangers sought.

"But we have a Holy Man here," said one of the women proudly. He is skin and bone, and fasts all the time when his old mother will let him."

But the strangers were not looking for a Holy Man however great his sanctity.

"At least inquire of him," one of the women insisted. "He might know of such a thing as you seek."

So they went to the Holy Man's croft; but he was lost in his Vision and for some time did not even hear what they were saying to him.

Then he was angry and said:

"Do not go astray after heathen Goddesses. Not after the Scarlet Woman of Babylon, nor after the Abominations of the Phoenicians. There is only one Redeemer, and that is the Living Son of God."

So the strangers went away, but the Holy Man's mother ran secretly after them.

"Do not be angry," she begged. "My son was not meaning to be discourteous to you; but he is so pure and so holy himself that he lives in a region far above this earth. He is a good man and a good son to me."

The strangers spoke kindly to her.

"We are not offended. You are a good woman, and have a good son."

"I am a very ordinary woman," she said. "But I must tell you that you should not believe in all these Aphrodites and Astartes and whatever their heathen names are. There is only one God, our Father in Heaven."

"You say you are only an ordinary woman," said the older of the two strangers. "But although your face is old and ravaged with the lines of sorrow, yet to my mind you have a face of great beauty—and I in my time was apprenticed to a great sculptor, so I know what beauty is."

Mary, amazed, cried out: "Once, perhaps, when I wove the coloured tapestry in the Temple, or when I poured my husband's wine in the shop, and held my first-born son in my arms. But *now*!"

But the old sculptor shook his head.

"Beauty lies beneath the skin," he insisted. "In the bone. Yes, and beneath that again—in the heart. So I say that you are a beautiful woman, perhaps more beautiful now than you were as a young girl. Farewell—and may you be blessed."

So the strangers rowed away in their boat, and Mary went slowly back to the croft and to her son.

The coming of the strangers had made him restless. He was walking up and down and his hands clasped his head in suffering.

Mary ran to him and held him in her arms.

"What is it, dear son?"

He groaned out: "The spirit has gone out of me . . . I am empty . . . empty . . . I am cut off from God—from the joy of his Presence."

Then she comforted him—as she had comforted him many times before, saying: "From time to time, this has to be—we do not know why. It is like the wave of the sea. It goes out from the shore, but it returns, my son, it returns."

But he cried out:

"You do not *know*. You cannot understand . . . You do not know what it is to be caught up in the Spirit, to be exalted with the great glory of God!"

And Mary said humbly:

"That is true. *That,* I have not felt. For me, there has been only memory. . . ."

"Memory is not enough!"

But Mary said fiercely: "It is enough for me!"

And she went to the door and stood there, looking out over the sea where the strangers had gone away. . . .

As she stood there, she felt a strange expectancy rising in her; a fluttering hopeful joy. Almost, she went down to the shore again, but she restrained herself, for she knew that her son would soon need her. And so it was. He began to shake all over, and his body jerked, and at last his limbs stiffened and he fell to the ground and lay like one dead. Then she covered him over for warmth and placed a fold of the cloak between his lips, in case the convulsions should come back. But he lay there motionless, and there was no sign, even, that he breathed.

Mary knew from experience that he would not stir for many hours, and she walked out again on to the hillside. It was growing dark now and the moon was rising over the sea.

Mary stood there savouring the welcome coolness of the evening. Her mind was full of memories of the past, of a hurried flight into Egypt, of the carpenter's shop, and of a marriage in Cana. . . .

And again that joyous expectancy rose in her.

"Perhaps," she thought," perhaps at last the time has come."

Presently, very slowly, she began to walk down to the sea. . . .

The moon rose in the sky, and it made a silvery path across the water, and as the light grew stronger, Mary saw a boat approaching.

She thought: "The strangers are coming back again. . . ."

But it was not the strangers . . . She could see now that it was not the handsome carved boat of the strangers. This was a rough fishing boat—the kind of boat that had been familiar to her all her life. . . .

And then she knew—quite certainly . . . It was *his* boat and he had come for her at last. . . .

And now she ran, slipping and stumbling over the rough stones of the beach. And as she reached the water's edge, half sobbing and half panting, she saw one of the three men step out of the boat onto the sea and walk along the moonlit path towards her.

Nearer and nearer he came . . . and then—and then . . . she was clasped in his arms . . . Words poured from her, incoherently, trying to tell so much.

"I have done as you asked me—I have looked after John—He has been as a son to me. I am not clever—I cannot always understand his high thoughts and his visions, but I have made him good food, and washed his feet, and tended him and loved him . . . I have been his mother and he has been my son. . . ?"

She looked anxiously up into his face, asking him a question.

"You have done all I asked you," he said gently. "Now—you are coming home with me."

"But how shall I get to the boat?"

"We will walk together on the water."

She peered out to sea.

"Are those—yes, they are—Simon and Andrew, are they not?"

"Yes, they wanted to come."

"How happy—Oh! how happy we are going to be," cried Mary. "Do you remember the day of the marriage in Cana. . . ?"

And so, walking together on the water, she poured out to her son all the little events and happenings of her life, and even how two strangers had come that very day looking for the "Queen of Heaven." And how ridiculous it was!

"They were quite right," said her Son. "The Queen of Heaven was here on the island, but they did not know her when they saw her. . . ."

And he looked into the worn, ravaged, beautiful face of his mother, and repeated softly:

"No, they did not know her when they saw her!"

In the morning, John awoke and rose from the ground.

It was the Lord's Day, and at once he knew that this was to be the great day of his life!

The Spirit rushed into him. . . .

He took up his pen and wrote:

I saw a new heaven and a new earth . . . And behind me I heard a great voice as of a trumpet . . . Saying:

I am Alpha and Omega, the first and the last . . . I am he that liveth and was dead; and behold, I am alive for evermore, Amen; and have the keys of hell and of death . . . Behold, I come quickly; and my reward is with me, to give every man according as his work shall be. . . .

THE ROAD OF DREAMS

A Masque from Italy

THE PLAYERS

PUNCHINELLO   HARLEQUIN   PIERROT

PULCINELLA   COLUMBINE   PIERRETTE

THE COMEDY OF THE ARTS

PROLOGUE: SUNG BY COLUMBINE

HARLEQUIN'S SONG

PIERROT'S SONG TO THE MOON

PIERRETTE DANCING ON THE GREEN

COLUMBINE'S SONG

PULCINELLA

THE SONG OF PIERROT BY THE HEARTH

THE LAST SONG OF COLUMBINE

PIERROT GROWN OLD

EPILOGUE: SPOKEN BY PUNCHINELLO

THE PROLOGUE:
SUNG BY COLUMBINE

HIGH on the hills and over the plains,
    A thousand years ago,
Hand in hand, and side by side,
Here with a skip, and there with a glide,
Together we went the wide world through,
    A thousand years ago.
Invisible spirits throughout the land,
Side by side, and hand in hand,
Harlequin and Columbine
    A thousand years ago!

HARLEQUIN'S SONG

I PASS
Where'er I've a mind,
With a laugh as I dance,
And a leap so high,
With a lightning glance,
And a crash and a flash
In the summer sky!
I come in the wind,
And I go with a sigh . . .
       And nobody ever sees Harlequin,
        Happy-go-lucky Harlequin,
Go by. . . .

(But never again with Columbine,
Never again with you.
Side by side, and hand in hand,
We wandered the wide world through!
And because I could not understand,
Columbine
Will never be mine,
Will never again be mine. . . .)

I come
With a tap on the cheek,
And a quip so gay,
An invisible sprite
In my motley array,
With a dangle o' spangle
To flash in the light!
And lo! when they seek—
I have vanished from sight!

    For nobody ever sees Harlequin,
    Happy-go-lucky Harlequin,
In flight. . . .

(But never again with Columbine,
Never again with you.
For with all the craft of my magic art
I never guessed what she loved the best
Was the song of a human heart. . . .
I gave her the earth, and the stars above,
And she bartered them all for a song of love!
A song that I never knew. . . .
So Columbine
Will never be mine,
Will never again be mine. . . .)

I pass
With a call and a cry
And a taunt so gay,

Like the flash of a dart
I speed on my way!
In a hush, with the rush
Of my magic art!
And I cannot die,

I must play my part. . . .
    For never a soul has Harlequin,
    Happy-go-lucky Harlequin,
Only a broken heart. . . .

PIERROT'S SONG TO THE MOON

I AM Pierrot, simple Pierrot, singing to the moon
Loving, longing, craving, crying,
Ever seeking, ever sighing,
Through the night to noon.
I am he all lovers know!
Wandering through the world I go
     In search of Columbine. . . .

I am Pierrot, lovelorn Pierrot, seeking Columbine!
As I see her in my dreaming,
She is fair beyond all seeming,
Gentle and divine. . . .
And I wander through life's ways,
Living lonely all my days,
     For love of Columbine!

Pierrette calls me, laughing Pierrette, with a merry cry:
"Pierrot! here is love and laughter!
Take no heed for what comes after,
Put your moon dreams by!
Come and dance! The world is wide!

You'll forget you ever sighed
    For love of Columbine!"

I am Pierrot, wand'ring Pierrot, passing on my way.

Though my love be never told her,

Though my arms shall never hold her,

I am hers alway.

Every lover knows my cry!

I go singing till I die
    For love of Columbine. . . .

PIERRETTE DANCING
ON THE GREEN

PIERRETTE dancing on the green
    Merrily, so merrily!
Curls of gold, and smile so sweet,
    And her eyes
    Are blue as skies
    The bluest ever seen!
Oh! never a care has gay Pierrette!
Only a pair of dancing feet,
    Dancing on the green.

"Pierrot, come and dance with me
    Merrily, so merrily!
Must you ever sigh and seek?
    Columbine
    May be divine,
    Yours she'll never be!
But ever a smile has gay Pierrette,
Rosebud mouth and a dimpled cheek!
    Come and dance with me."
Pierrette dancing far and near
    Daintily, so daintily!

If we never more should meet,
    Would your eyes
    As blue as skies
    Shed a single tear?
Oh! never a heart has gay Pierrette!
Only a pair of dancing feet,
    Dancing far and near.

"Handsome Pierrot, go your way
    Wearily, so wearily!
Sing of dove-eyed Columbine,
    Tears I leave
    For her to grieve,
    I go ever gay!
Oh! many a swain has fair Pierrette!
Many a foot to follow mine!
    Pierrot! Go your way."

Pierrette dancing on the green
    Merrily, so merrily!
Curls of gold, and smile so sweet,
    And her eyes
    Are blue as skies
    The bluest ever seen!
Oh! never a care has gay Pierrette!
Only a pair of dancing feet,
    Dancing on the green.

COLUMBINE'S
SONG

PIERROT singing to the moon
    For love of me. . . .
And his singing
Goes on ringing,
Softly clinging
    To my heart. . . .
        Harlequin! Your magic art,
        Reaching to the skies above,
        Circling round the world so free,
        Never made a song of love . . .
            A song of love for me. . . .

Pierrot singing to the moon
    "Alack is me!"
And his breaking
Heart is making,
Softly waking
    Love unknown. . . .
        Harlequin! Go on alone.
        I will lead a mortal life,

Toil and spin in poverty.
Come now, Sorrow, Pain and Strife,
And Pierrot's love for me.

Pierrot singing to the moon
For love of me. . . .
Ages welling
Find me dwelling,
Ne'er rebelling,
By his fire.
Harlequin! by my desire
I have won a soul at last.
I forget when I was free,
I forget the days long past
Ere Pierrot sang to me. . . .

PULCINELLA

ONCE upon a time, they say,
 (Listen how it chanced,)
Punchinello pulled the strings
 And Pulcinella danced!

All the world's a puppet show,
 (Queen of Puppets, I!)
Silk and satin is my wear,
See my richly braided hair!
Bought and sold
For love of gold,
 Queen of Puppets, I!

Long ago I had a heart, and sighed alas! alack!
(Pierrot, cease your singing, lest you bring remembrance back.)
Long ago I had a soul, innocent and wise,
(Columbine, oh, turn aside, I dare not meet your eyes.)
Long ago I laughed and danced, youthful on the green!
(Pierrette, stay your dancing, lest I mourn for what has been.)

For my heart is dead at last,
And my soul died in the past,

And my youth is dying fast . . .
Poor painted Pulcinella!

All the world's a puppet show,
    (I, the Puppet Queen!)
Love I scorned and passed it by,
Rainbow-tinted fragile tie,
Gold I sought,
And gold I bought,
    I, the Puppet Queen!

Once upon a time, they say,
    (Listen how it chanced,)
Punchinello pulled the string,
The olden string,
The golden string,
    And Pulcinella danced!

THE SONG
OF PIERROT BY
THE HEARTH

COLUMBINE sits by my fire!
She is mine! She is mine!
Columbine!

Can a lover's heart, then, never
Rest content, but must it ever
Still go caring, grieving, fearing . . .
Tremble with delight and dread
Lest some day I find her fled . . . ?
Watch her, when the fire burns low,
Start up with a sudden cry!
      (Well, I know what she is hearing,
          Harlequin is passing by. . . .)

Lightning flashes up above!
      (Memories waken in her eyes,
        Memories I do not know)
And the love-light slowly dies. . . .
Harlequin can hold her so!
Harlequin has every art!

Pierrot but his longing heart . . .
 And his song of love!

Courage, Pierrot, courage yet!
Up! and sing to her again,
All your passion and your pain. . . .
She shall listen—listen yet—
She shall listen and forget
 That Harlequin goes by. . . .

I am Pierrot, simple Pierrot, singing
 to the moon!
Loving, longing, craving, crying,
Ever fearing, ever sighing,
Through the night to noon.
Every lover hears my cry,
I go singing till I die,
 For love of Columbine. . . .

THE LAST SONG OF
COLUMBINE

FIRE on the hills, and fire on the plain,
    As a thousand years ago
A sudden breeze from a far-off strand,
Magic around me that once I knew
When side by side, and hand in hand,
        Went Harlequin and Columbine,
        A thousand years ago.

Memory wakes . . . and memory dies . . .
Magic around me that swiftly flies,
A breath on my cheek that I understand,
A sob and a cry, and a laugh sky-high!
It is Harlequin, Harlequin, passing by!
        Harlequin passing by!

Oh! to be out and wandering free,
By hill and by plain, and by moonlit sea,
As once I went—ah! me—ah! me,
        A thousand years ago!

Shatter the walls that hem me in!
Scatter the children before the door!

Let me go out and roam as before,
Out from the hearth and the firelit home
Into the starry night to roam,
As I roamed with Harlequin!

Fire on the hills, and fire on the plain,
    (And Harlequin passing by),
The rustle of leaves by an unseen hand,
The lilt of a song, we sang, we two . . .
A stifled sob—and a touch on my hand . . .
    And Harlequin goes by. . . .

PIERROT GROWN OLD

HERE upon the hearth together,
Here, where once the children played,
I and Pierrette watch together,
I and Pierrette undismayed.
Hand in hand we played as children,
In the bygone days of old,
Now we watch the shadows lengthen,
I and Pierrette—growing old. . . .

Pierrette's hand has left the blind
Half unlatched, and, from behind
Darkening clouds, *there shines the moon.* . . .
    (On the hearth the ashes flicker,
    Pierrot, does your heart beat quicker?
    Even now in grey December,
    As you look, and you remember
    Earlier days when you went singing,
    Set the whole wide world a-ringing
    With your song of love and pain?)
Turn you back to where the ember
Strangely kindled dies again . . .

Shun the moon lest you remember
  Columbine, who died so soon. . . .

Something stirring in the garden . . .
Some soft footfall on the grass. . . .
  (What takes Pierrot to the window,
  Watching whose light foot shall pass?)
Flash of spangle in the moonlight!
Crash of thunder! Lightning gleam!
Is it two who dance together
As immortals in a dream?
  (Dreaming only brings one pain,
  Can the dead return again?)
Hark! a step upon the pathway!
Hush! a hand upon the door!
Then the door swings slowly open,
There's a step upon the floor . . .
Just a rustle and a sigh,
There beside me—close, close by . . .
Some wild bird flown in for shelter?
No! for I could swear I felt her
Tender lips on mine . . .
Bringing back to me again
All the splendour and the pain!
  It is Columbine. . . .

Crash! the door blows to again!
Dark the room and strangely cold . . .
Pierrette, rising from her seat,

Pulls the blind with sudden heat,
Shuts the moon from out my sight
    (*Pierrette ever hates its light*)!
Is there anger in her eyes?
Knowledge, fear, and swift surprise?
     (*Strange the room should turn so cold* . . .
     Pierrot! You are growing old. . . .)
She and I the selfsame folk
Bound together by the yoke
Of the common years together . . .
Through the fair or clouded weather.
So shall we, the selfsame clay,
Watch the ashes growing grey. . . .

Lead me back, then, where the fire
Gives one leap of last desire!
Flickers faint and fitful yet,
    As a heart that would forget. . . .
Moon-dreams only bring one pain!
Can the dead return again?
    Columbine died in the past . . .
    And the fire burns out at last. . . .

EPILOGUE:
SPOKEN BY PUNCHINELLO

THE Play is done! The Tale is told!

Off masks, and bow
Before you pass your way!
Comes the old Showman now
And speaks his lines as best he may.
Buffoon is he, well known and loved of old,
A pleasant wag, a merry fellow!
Oh! all the world loves Punchinello!

> *Touch my hump for luck, sirs!*
> *Laugh and laugh again!*
> *If I cannot make you laugh,*
> *What's the good of pain?*

She I loved in days of old
Wedded me for love of gold.
If I dreamed her heart was mine,
True as that of Columbine,
Soon the veil was torn aside,
Puppet heart, and puppet bride!

Just a painted puppet thing,
Dancing on a golden string!

Touch my hump for luck, then,
Touch and come again!
If I cannot make you laugh,
What's the good of pain?

Harlequin and Columbine
Dance through life without a sign,
And no more upon the green
Pierrette's dancing feet are seen.
No one knows why Pierrot sighs—
Punchinello never dies. . . .
Simple mirth and homely jest!
So the children loved him best.

Men and women play you false,
But until the end,
He who makes the children laugh,
Is the children's friend!

The Tale is told! The Play is o'er!
The Lines are said!
The Puppets pass their way . . .
Their names may fade
But they themselves shall live alway,
And they shall play the parts they played before,
While Time shall make the Play more mellow,
So listen now to Punchinello:

Where'er a lover sings and sighs, there Pierrot lives again,
Beneath the moon, he passes by, and pours out all his pain.
As long as youth and mirth endure, there Pierrette may be seen,
While many a footstep follows hers a-dancing on the green.
And oh! as long as gold is gold, and money chinks and rings,
There Pulcinella dances when you pull the golden strings;
While every man, for weal or woe, goes seeking Columbine,
Immortal soul imprisoned in a woman's eyes divine.
And when the fire burns low at night, and lightning flashes high!
Then guard your hearth, and hold your love, for Harlequin
    goes by.

And lastly, where the children play, until the very end,
You'll find old Punchinello, whom they call the children's friend!

> *Touch my hump for luck, dears!*
> *Laugh and laugh again!*
> *If I cannot make you laugh,*
> *What's the good of pain?*

Ballads

The Ballad of the Flint

THE Flint, it was our Weapon! The Circle was our Home!
The Tors closed in around us, and we never dared to roam.
The Flint, it was our Weapon, and we kept the Beasts at bay,
When there came on us the Sea Men—the roving Northern
        Free Men,
And closed in all around us, as we fled in wild dismay!

They had Knives of Magic Metal! Their beards were flaming red!
But one there was, a mighty man, o'ertopped them by a head.
He cried: "Well done, my Vikings, we will leave them limb and
        life,
Take their cattle, we require them—take their wives if you desire
        them.
As for me, who am your Captain, now be mine the Headman's
        wife!"

A groan came from the People (She was our Eyes and Ears),
The Phoenician blood flowed in her from down the longpast
        years.
Alone, she stood there fearless. "O Stranger from the Sea,
Take back thy hand and leave me; my Eyes cannot deceive me!
It is Doom of Death I bring thee . . . so be warned and let me be!"

But he laughed a mighty laugh, and he swore aloud by Thor:
"From thy cringing mate I take thee, to be mine for evermore,
For the magic of thy presence, for the beauty of thy face!"
Then they strode across the valleys, to the Sea Coast and their
    galleys,
And they took her bound amongst them, to our shame and our
    disgrace.

Then the Headman called the People—far and near they came in
    flocks,
And a mighty tempest, raging, drove the galleys on the rocks.
Bruised and spent we found the Sea Men (and we praised the
    holy Sun!)
In confusion there we found them, and we seized and held and
    bound them,
And we slew them there with laughter! Yea, we slew them—all
    save *One*!

With a taunt the Headman mocked him, as he cut the woman
    free:
"We will spare thee for the torture of the slowest death there be!"
But the woman spoke out proudly: "*I* am Priestess of the Sun!
Come, ye People all, and follow to the Sacrificial Hollow
Where I strike the Blow of Vengeance! It is thus it shall be done!"

The Woman was our Priestess. We followed where she led
To the Secret Hollow in the Rocks where Human Blood is shed.
And we cast the Victim down there—but he called her by her
    name:

"Is thy heart, then, as unyielding as the Flint Stone thou art
    wielding?

Or is it as our Northern Iron—which melts in fiercest flame. . . ?"

"I am Priestess of the Circle. To the Headman I am wife.

Dost thou understand, O Stranger, that our God must have thy
    life?"

And he answered: "Strike, then, gladly—since my death comes by
    thy hand!

And I would thy Gods were my Gods—the only true and high
    Gods!"

Then she smiled—and struck unflinching! (But we did not
    understand.)

"O Sun God of our People, Whose Eyes and Ears I be!

My blow, it has avenged Thee—Thy Priestess now is free!

So I turn to Thor and Odin—They who guard the Northern
    foam.

Let my Stranger Lover meet me! In thy Valhall let him greet me!"

The Flint (it is our Weapon)—to her heart she struck it home!

Elizabeth of England

I AM Mistress of England—the Seas I hold!
    I have gambled, and won, alone. . . .
I have freed my land from the power of Spain,
I have gathered in gold from the Spanish Main
With the help of my mariners bold.
    But never a child of my flesh and blood,
    When I shall be dead and gone,
    Oh! never a King of the Tudor blood
    Shall sit upon England's throne. . . .

        I have saved my land from the dreaded foe,
        My fleet will be known to fame,
        And many a ship has sailed to the West
        In Gloriana's name!

I was menaced by Spain before I was born
    In the months, oh! mother most dear,
When my father defied those powers twain,
The curse of the Church and the might of Spain,
To keep the oath he had sworn!
    And Katharine, raging, invoked her God,
    And appealed both far and near,

And fostered the plan of leer and of nod
Which brought you down to the bier. . . .

So is it written in ages past
    With a woman's smile as bait,
A King shall risk his very soul
And change a nation's fate. . . .

Did you never fear, oh! mother of mine,
    When you played on a King's desire,
When first of a queenly rank you dreamed,
And subtly plotted and boldly schemed
To further your high design?
    Did you never dread that the hand which crowned
    Could cast you down in the mire,
    That a love so swift might be swiftly drowned,
    And a King might love—and tire?

        Oh! red were your lips as you smiled in his face,
        And red was your hair as fire!
        And red was the band around your neck
        As you met your doom so dire. . . .

An Oath I swore!—and the Pride of Spain
    Is driftwood along my coast!
I was not too royal to scheme and to smile,
To pay with a promise—and dally awhile—
Till I changed my mind again. . . .

Your blood, oh! mother, which gave me might,
(Not that of the Tudor host,)
And a woman's game that was played aright
Is Elizabeth Tudor's boast.

'Tis perilous work to trifle with France . . .
To jest with Spain may be death . . .
But I played my part with a woman's guile
And never a catch in my breath!

I have hated most women—but *one* above all,
(No matter her rank or name,)
Fair was her face, and her fame spread wide
When in France she dwelt as a royal bride
Ere she sailed to her fate and fall.
The lure of her beauty drew all mankind
Like a moth to the candle flame . . .
They brought me the warrant to sign . . . and I signed
With a flourish my royal name!

(But oh! to think that when I am gone
And laid in my grave so low,
The Crown which rests on my royal head
Shall adorn a Stewart's false brow!)

She had fostered a plan to seize my throne,
Conspiring with Rome and Spain,
She had aimed at my life, so they said—what then?
It was never fear that drove my pen!

(*Who have never a child of my own . . .*)
>But the jealous rage that naught can slake
>Of a woman who loved in vain . . .
>And she shall die for her beauty's sake!
>Who has loved—and been loved again!

>>(There are gallants thronging around my throne,
>>And many a maiden fair,
>>But the maids who come to Elizabeth's court
>>Must coif Saint Catherine's hair!)

I am Queen of England! I rule unafraid!
>(But never a son of my own . . .)
I have gowns in plenty, and jewels rare,
With many a wench to tire my hair,
And they call me a painted jade!
>But many a ship in Elizabeth's name
>Shall open up seas unknown. . . .
>*And I shall share in my Children's fame*
>*Who have never a child of my own. . . .*

The Bells of Brittany

BELLS are ringing o'er the sea,
  The gentle bells of Brittany.
Rock the cradle to and fro,
Croon a lullaby so low,
Mark the cross upon her brow,
She is Christ's for ever now.
    (White thy tiny hands, my dove,
    Small and white and made for love.
    Love to wake, and love to keep . . .)
    Rock the cradle, let her sleep,
While the bells ring out and say
That a child was born today!

Bells are tolling o'er the sea,
  The woeful bells of Brittany.
Rock the cradle lest she wake,
Learn who died for her sweet sake.
Mark a cross upon that brow,
Which shall sleep for ever now.
    (Dark thy downy head, my sweet,
    Motherless the world to meet,

Fold thy little hands in sleep . . .)
Rock the cradle lest she weep,
While the bells toll on and say
That a mother died today. . . .

Isolt of Brittany

My Lord and I upon a hill
Looked out across the sea
And watched the gulls that wheel and turn
And circle endlessly.

And Lo, my Lord was lost in thought
Until to him I said:
"Thy thoughts are very far away
From her thou soon shalt wed.

"In Cornwall, at Queen Isolt's court
The maids are fair to see
Fairer are they, my Lord, perchance
Than those of Brittany."

Then Tristan stayed in thought awhile,
Then smiled and answered me:
"There is no maid at Isolt's court
One half as fair as thee."

My Lord and I upon a hill
Looked out to sea a while.

I doubt not . . . yet I would I knew
What lay behind his smile . . .

My Lord and I in Brittany
Looked out across the sea,
And oh, his thoughts, his wand'ring thoughts,
Were far away from me.

Dark Sheila

SHEILA, dark Sheila, what is it that you're seeing?
What is it that you're seeing, that you're seeing in the fire?
I see a lad that loves me . . . And I see a lad that leaves me . . .
And a third lad, a Shadow Lad . . . (and he's the lad that grieves me)
And whatever I am seeing,
There's no fearing and no fleeing . . .
But whatever I am seeing, it is not my heart's desire. . . .

Sheila, dark Sheila, with whom will you be roaming?
With whom will you be roaming when the summer day has
    flown?
A lad there is who loved me—but loves me now no longer,
A lad there is who left me (and oh! his love grows stronger!)
But wherever I go roaming,
You shall never find me homing,
For wherever I go roaming, I must wander all alone. . . .

"Sheila, dark Sheila, will you listen to my pleading?
Will you listen to my pleading, will you recompense my pain?
For I'm the lad who loved you, the lad who so deceived you.
I left you for another girl, and oh! I fear I grieved you!
But if you'll hear my pleading

As across the moor you're speeding,
Oh! if you'll hear my pleading, I'll return to you again."

"Sheila, dark Sheila, will you hearken to my calling?
Will you hearken to my calling, as I call from far away?
For I'm the lad that left you (but never could forget you),
And I'm the lad that loved you from the very hour he met you!
And if you'll hear my calling
As the shades of night are falling,
Oh! if you'll hear my calling, I'll be yours alone alway!"

But Sheila, dark Sheila, is out upon the moorland.
She's out upon the moorland where the heather meets the sky!
And the lads shall never find her, for there's one walks by her side
there,
A Stranger Lad, a Shadow Lad, who would not be denied
there. . . .
She turned her to his calling
As the shades of night were falling,
She turned her to his calling . . . and she answered to his Cry. . . .

Ballad of the Maytime

THE King, he went a-walking, one merry morn in May.
The King, he laid him down to rest, and fell asleep, they say.
>   And when he woke, 'twas even,
>   (The hour of magic mood,)
And Bluebell, wild Bluebell, was dancing in the wood.

The King, he gave a banquet to all the flowers (save one),
With hungry eyes he watched them, a-seeking one alone.
>   The Rose was there in satin,
>   The Lily with green hood,
But Bluebell, wild Bluebell, only dances in the wood.

The King, he frowned in anger, his hand upon his sword.
He sent his men to seize her, and bring her to their Lord.
>   With silken cords they bound her,
>   Before the King she stood,
Bluebell, wild Bluebell, who dances in the wood.

The King, he rose to greet her, the maid he'd sworn to wed.
The King, he took his golden crown and set it on her head.
>   And then he paled and shivered,
>   The courtiers gazed in fear,
At Bluebell, grey Bluebell, so pale and ghostly there.

"O King, your crown is heavy, 'twould bow my head with care.
Your palace walls would shut me in, who live as free as air.

    The wind, he is my lover,

    The sun my lover too,

And Bluebell, wild Bluebell, shall ne'er be Queen to you."

The King, he mourned a twelvemonth, and none could ease his
    pain.
The King, he went a-walking a-down a lovers' lane.

    He laid aside his golden crown,

    Into the wood went he,

Where Bluebell, wild Bluebell, dances ever wild and free.

The Princess Sings

BRING me my lute and let me play
A bygone ballad of yesterday.

Four knights there were from far away
(Ring out, my lute, on a chord so gay!)
Four knights who came to kiss my hand
From the East and the West
And the far Northland.
      And one from the South . . .
      Who kissed my mouth . . .
      And stole my heart away. . . .

Bring me my lute and let me sing
A ballad of yore with the old gay ring.

Out in the West the sun dies red
(Where does my true love lay his head?)
Four knights who came from o'er the sea,
One I hold, and one holds me.
And one I never again shall see . . .

Who came from the South
And kissed my mouth,
And stole my heart away. . . .

Lost in the West is the setting sun,
Take then my lute, the tale is done!

Dreams and Fantasies

The Dream Spinners

Oh! who shall see the Spinners?
The silent white-robed Spinners?
The tender cruel Spinners
    As they spin the Thread of Dreams?

    Can you hear the Wheel a-whirring?
    And the menace of its purring?
    See the colour of a rainbow as it gleams?
    Can you see the shining mesh
    That is spun for human flesh?
    Can you hear them?
    Do you fear them?
    Will you dare to wander near them?
        The silent white-robed Spinners
    As they spin the Web of Dreams. . . .

The conqueror from the battle by their gleam is led astray,
Where the fragile threads enfold him—there his armour rusts
        away. . . .
The boy who goes a-ploughing at the dusky hour of eve
Sees a Vision grey and golden—and his furrow he must
        leave.

And the maiden in the village, who has knelt beside the lake,

And has seen a Dream-face pictured—goes unwedded for

      his sake. . . .

    Oh! if your eyes shall see them,

    You had better turn and flee them,

    For no power born of earth shall hold you then.

    And you'll let the world go by,

    Seeking Beauty till you die!

    If you hear them,

    Oh! beware them!

    And never venture near them!

      The silent white-robed Spinners

    As they spin the Thread of Dreams. . . .

There are Threads of Red and Golden! There are Threads of Grey

      and Green!

There are Threads of White and Silver. And they merge in

      dazzling sheen!

There's a Web of wondrous weaving that is Rose and Amethyst,

And a Purple Strand of Mystery that fades into the mist. . . .

And oh! there's love and longing! There's a heart to laugh and

      grieve,

There's Wonder . . . and there's Pity—where the white-robed

      Spinners weave. . . .

    Oh! who shall find the Spinners?

    The silent white-robed Spinners?

    The tender cruel Spinners

      As they spin the Web of Dreams. . . .

Down in the Wood

BARE brown branches against a blue sky
    (*And Silence within the wood*),
Leaves that, listless, lie under your feet,
Bold brown boles that are biding their time
    (*And Silence within the wood*).
Spring has been fair in the fashion of youth,
Summer with languorous largesse of love,
Autumn with passion that passes to pain,
Leaf, flower, and flame—they have fallen and failed

    And Beauty—bare Beauty is left in the wood!

Bare brown branches against a mad moon
    (*And Something that stirs in the wood*),
Leaves that rustle and rise from the dead,
Branches that beckon and leer in the light
    (*And Something that walks in the wood*).
Skirling and whirling, the leaves are alive!
Driven by Death in a devilish dance!
Shrieking and swaying of terrified trees!
A wind that goes sobbing and shivering by . . .

    And Fear—naked Fear passes out of the wood!

The Road of Dreams

The Road of Dreams leads up the Hill
      So straight and white
    And bordered wide
    With almond trees on either side
    In rosy flush of Spring's delight!
    Against the frown
    Of branches brown
    The blossoms laugh and gleam,
        Within my dream. . . .

There is no Joy like Joy in Dreams . . .
      Up—up the Hill
    My flying feet
    Go magically winged and fleet
    And like a bird that flies at will!
    So shall I find
    What God designed
    There—where the Open Country lies
        Before my eyes. . . .

There is no Fear like Fear in Dreams . . .
>Which, swift as Death

Pursuing fast,

Gains on me, till I feel at last

Upon my neck its icy breath. . . .

The Dream is dead!

The Joy is fled!
>The Road of Dreams

Leads up the Hill and faintly gleams. . . .

Oh! Dream most fond,

What lies beyond?
>*Beyond the Hill. . . .*

Heritage

THE South Wind comes a–whispering, a–whispering from the Sea,
And tells of waters cool and clear,
Of far off strands
With golden sands
And Halcyon days to be.
And oh! there's life a-stirring at the very heart of me
That listens to the South Wind, to the South Wind from the Sea.

The Forest comes a-murmuring, a-murmuring all around,
And speaks of magic dark and sweet,
Of charms untold,
Enchantments old,
Of nymphs with hair unbound . . .
And oh! the life a-stirring, it quivers at the sound,
It quivers at the murmur of the Forest all around.

There's a Voice that comes a-calling, a-calling from the Lea:
"Who walks with Me in wind and storm,
He knows no rest
But only zest
God's great wide world to see!"
And oh! the life that's stirring, it struggles to be free
As it hears the Voice a-calling, a-calling from the Lea!

The Wanderer

In the dark woods I shall find peace!
There shall I learn at last
Forgetfulness!
    Or, if that may not be,
    I will remember what is past
    Most joyfully!

On the high hills where once I went,
I shall not come again
Triumphantly!
    But it remains for me
    To laugh into the face of pain
    Defiantly!

By the deep seas I dwelt content,
There, by your side,
In harmony . . .
    Now there is left for me
    Naught but to face the incoming tide
    Courageously!

In the dark grave there lies release,
There shall I sleep anew
Nor wake again. . . .
    And if that shall not be,
    I will remember only you,
    And live as you would have me do
    Most valiantly!

The Dream City

I KNOW a city where black lions dwell
And guard a fountain in a giant square.
The City rises round it, white and proud.
The streets are broad and wide—and you and I
Walk there together, gladly, side by side;
We go in silence—speak no word, but each
The other's thought has understood and heard. . . .
Our feet seem not to touch the ground, so swift
And fleet we speed together on our way.
Between us there is understanding. Ay!
And all around is Beauty—also Peace. . . .
It is a dream. . . . But oh! when Life shall cease,
And many thousand years have passed away,
We may be born again, perchance, and dwell
In that great city built by mightier men
Who toiling through long centuries, have learnt
To banish Pain. . . . It may be so—who knows . . . ?
It may be you and I shall live again. . . .

A Passing

A WHIRLING of dead leaves,
A gathering in of sheaves,
The stripping of the trees,
The ebbing of the seas,
The shifting of the sands,
A vision of far lands. . . .
A sundering and a thundering
Of prison bars that fall!
The answer to a call
New destiny to shape . . .
A silence . . . and a breath. . . .
We call it—Death!
Nor dare to say—Escape!

Other Poems

Über Poesie.

Spring

A CHILD has passed through the woods today,
Hush! You shall find him there at play!
See—snowdrops scattered in the glade,
And nestling close in childlike grace,
The crocus lifts his chubby face,
Serene and unafraid!
And out on the downs
In their straight green gowns
The daffodils wait. . . . Whilst hidden quite
The shy blue violets in delight
Peer forth to tempt his careless hand . . .
And the Child who passes by today goes laughing through
the land!

A Child has passed through the city street,
Follow the track of his little feet . . .
Golden-hued baskets on the curb,
A lifted head and a brightened eye
As the busy worker passes by
And the flowers his thoughts disturb. . . .
A sudden stir
In the wintry air!

A tired heart that knows a gleam

Of strange sweet joy . . . A transient dream

Of all the things that might have been. . . .

> And a Child who passes through the street—who passes all
>
> unseen. . . .

Stay, Child! What is thy name?

Whence art thou come? Who gave thee birth?

> *My Mother, the Earth*
>
> *Bore me in joy!*
>
> *She, the All Wise*
>
> *Fashioned my limbs*
>
> *In this fair guise*
>
> *Without alloy.*

Who is thy Father?

> *The Breath of a Flame!*
>
> *In the Future is written the Might of his Name. . . .*
>
> *Offspring am I of the Seen and Unseen,*
>
> *Of that which shall come, and of that which hath been!*
>
> *Wisdom of Ages—and Promise of Dawn,*
>
> *Calling to life all the life yet unborn,*
>
> *Lo! in the CHILD is the Hope of the Earth!*
>
> *So shall I pass—bringing Spring and Rebirth!*

Young Morning

Night gave me birth, and to my fashioning went
Fear and Unrest, Hate that will not relent,
Pain, and a Joy too keen to face the light,
Passion, Desire, and Mystery of Night . . .

A wreath of stars is set upon my brow,
And, twining round my feet, pale lilies grow,
My body has the beauty of the Moon,
Its slender whiteness girt with holy rune.

My heart is full of doubts that softly wake,
Longings not understood—the strange sweet ache
Of unfulfilled desire . . . Dreamful of Fate,
Veiled in my nightblack hair, I stand and wait!

This is my hour!
    Eternity itself halts on its ceaseless round,
    And all the world halts with it for a little spell,
    And in the quivering stillness comes the sound
    Of all the secret music that I love so well:
    The sighs of lovers, and the haunting cry
    Of tawny beasts, and the awakening call

Of drowsy baby birds in nests so high. . . .
My outspread arms rule over all!
This is my hour!

The stars around my head have paled away,
The lily buds are opening gold and gay,
From out the slumbering hills there cometh One
Most glorious without—within—the Sun!

About my limbs the purple mists unfold,
Upon my head—a Crown of Blood and Gold!
And I am wrapped in rich and varied hue,
Crimson and rose, and faintest starry blue. . . .

What is this strange new anguish in my heart?
See—where the mists of morning slowly part
My Lover comes! His banners bravely borne
And greets me in the burning Kiss of Dawn!

Give me my hour within my Lover's arms!
Vanished the doubts, the fears, the sweet alarms!
I lose myself within his quickening Breath. . . .
And when he tires and leaves me—there is Death. . . .

Hymn to Ra

From the West we came,
To the West we shall return!
>Ra! Giver of all! Listen and hear!
>Hark to Thy People's Oath! Thus do we swear!
>*We will return to the West*
>*There, to the Land of the Blest,*
>>There whence we came. . . .

From the West we came,
To the West we shall return!
>Ra! Light of the World! Keep our Faith pure!
>We are the chosen Race! We shall endure!
>Slaves are the Black and the White!
>Great are the Red in Thy sight!
>>Lords of the World!

From the West we came,
To the West we shall return!
>Ra! Red is Thy Light! Mighty Thy Heat!
>Thou shalt set every nation under our feet!
>We who are Builders in Stone,
>Forgers of Metal unknown,
>>Rulers of All!

From the West we came,
To the West we shall return!

Ra! We are Thy Sons! Thus 'tis decreed:

"With our own kind will we mate, we and our seed.

In whose veins runs the blood of a slave

He shall go down to the grave!"

Lest we grow weak.

From the West we came,
To the West we shall return!

Ra! Father of Strength! Thou who art Life!

Guide Thou our spears in the battle, prosper our Strife!

Yet, when the fight is o'er,

Let us return once more

Back to the West . . .

A Palm Tree in the Desert

In the Desert I stand
Alone—always alone . . .
Whilst around me the shifting sands
Change not from day to day.
And now and again from the far-off lands
Comes a breath that lifts my leaves
In unquenchable hope . . .
Then, sighing, they sink once more to their rest. . . .

Here by the pool in the Desert
The camels halt and kneel,
Patient and weary . . .
And the Men of the Desert turn to the East
At the hour of the Midday prayer.
Their weariness stayed and refreshed,
They pass from my sight far into the North,
And only the sands,
The shifting sands of the Desert
Are left. . . .

I have lived through one passionate hour!
Sirocco—Wind of the South—

Like an Avenger came!
Where he had passed
None lifted their heads again. . . .
He clasped me close,
Scorched by his breath,
Tortured in joy,
I gave myself up to be seared and devoured!
A mist of hot sand rose around us
Veiling us close. . . .
Then, like a Flame
Onward he rushed to the North
In that Column of whirling and eddying sand
Which is Death. . . .
Sirocco—Breath of the Desert!
When shalt thou come again?
Return! Return!

The day of Khamsen is past . . .
And I am left
Here by the pool in the Desert
Alone . . . always alone. . . .

World Hymn 1914

THUNDER of guns and clash of steel!
Fashion it out with lathe and with wheel.
These are the masters of men today,
Men who created, and men who pay.
    A hum in the sky
    Where the war birds fly,
Battle, murder, and sudden death,
Women who pray with a catch in their breath,
    The God of War is nigh!

Thunder of guns, and clash of steel!
Women who work, and women who kneel,
Crying aloud: "How long, how long?
Before the right shall defeat the wrong?"
    Silence and Peace,
    Rest and Release!
Hearts that are fainting beneath the strain
Call upon Heaven in passionate pain,
    Call to the God of Peace.

Thunder of guns, and clash of steel!
All the way through, for woe or for weal,

The throb of a People's heart that is breaking,

The stir of a People's soul that is waking . . .

    And beneath the roar

    Of the weapons of war,

A Silence set in the midst of Sound . . .

And a Voice that shall never again be drowned . . .

    The Unknown God is speaking. . . .

Easter 1918

Let us today know only great rejoicing,
Nor mourn our gallant dead, so young and gay
Like Easter flowers
That stand in youthful vigour straight and golden,
Those Easter flowers which fill the world today!
Let now be ours
The wider vision (though our eyes be holden)
The deeper understanding that shall see
Death as a change which comes at Life's beginning,
A joyous rushing of young souls set free. . . .

Let us not mar the splendour of their going!
Their loving and their laughter shall not cease.
So shall we almost hear, for ever growing
Out of the silent darkness day by day,
The rushing sound of a triumphant massing!
Oh! let us then acclaim that valiant passing
Which some call Death—and others name Release!

To a Beautiful Old Lady

DRIED roseleaves for your lips,
Grey ashes for your hair,
Cold sapphires for your shrewd old eyes
Which looked on life so calmly wise
And never knew a tear.

Old ivory for your arms
Which never held a child.
Your cheek is smooth as Dresden ware
     With ne'er a line to tell of care,
You—who have watched and smiled!

So Pain has passed you by,
And Love and Toil and Sin . . .
You've dwelt within a self-built wall,
And when the shell shall break and fall
There's emptiness within. . . .

Wild Roses

I know
Where the wild roses grow
   Beside the lake.
The little spirits come and play,
And pink and white
Dance in the light
Before the break of day!
The sun comes up in golden heat,
The roses open wide . . . and fall . . .
   And that is all . . .
Except I think I hear a sound
   Along the ground,
Of many little pattering feet. . . .

No more
Shall my wild rose of yore
   Walk by the lake.
She told me where the rose sprites were
And how they played
All undismayed
By her sweet presence there!
Then Death rose up twixt her and me!

She turned her, smiling, to his call . . .
And that is all . . .
Except I cannot bear to go
Where roses grow
Beside the lake—so wild and free. . . .

Love Passes

LOVE passes! On the hearth dead embers lie
Where once there burned a fire of living flame,
Where we, starved children, sheltering in shame,
Stretched out our hands, and let the world go by,
Warming our frozen hearts in ecstasy
And dreaming Love should always be the same. . . .
In vain your pity! And in vain my blame!
Love passes—and we know not whence or why. . . .

Love passes out into the silent night,
We may not hold him who has served our will
And, for a while, made magic common things. . . .
Now, like a bird, he spreads his wings in flight,
And we are left in darkness—listening still
To the faint far-off beating of his wings. . . .

Progression

LOVE comes as the Spring comes
Fearing . . .
Dreading . . .
The brown boughs are in blossom;
A breath of frost,
A wind from the leas,
And the blossom would fall . . .
But close to the earth
The tiny common flowers
Blossom unheeded . . .

Summer!
And love . . .
Stillness
And at the heart of the Stillness
A throb. . . .

Flame!
Flame in the Forest!
Flame in my heart!
Lover of mine
Never was love such as ours

Ecstasy . . .

Joy . . .

Passion . . .

Pain . . .

Closer, O heart of mine . . .

Closer yet . . .

Your lips . . .

In the Forest the leaves are on fire,

Spendthrift and reckless their joy!

Riot of life!

What was that strange dry sound?

A leaf that crackled beneath my feet

Withered and brown . . .

Closer, O heart of mine.

I am afraid . . .

Your lips. . . .

Wintertime

Peace

Dead heart

(Or asleep?)

A touch?

A kiss?

What are these that they leave me so cold?

Emptiness

Death. . . .

A bird in the wood,

Now do I surely know that I shall awake!

Return once more to love and delight,

Springtime will come again,

The almond trees blossom once more . . .

And yet I weep,

For never again shall I tread love's ways with you . . .

Farewell, O Lover of mine,

Our day is done.

Wintertime

Peace

O lover of mine that I loved,

Farewell. . . .

There Where My Lover Lies

THERE where my lover lies,
A King palm at his head,
The earth is warm and kind,
A little whispering wind
Comes from the hills,
Lingers in passing . . . and then dies . . .
There where my lover lies
Greeting the dead. . . .

No frangipani flow'rs,
Honeyed and sweet,
Shall mock our radiant hours,
But at his feet
Night blooming Cereus grows. . . .

You were a king, my love, and I
In the far North lie nightly down to die.
Then, on your grave, a thousand flowers are born,
Wide cups of white

Filled with delight,
Lasting their radiant hour to dawn!

There lies my lover—dead,
A King palm at his head,
Night Cereus at his feet,
The night is all too fleet. . . .

POEMS

Things

Beauty

THE earth is Beauty and also longing;
Without desire and incompleteness
There is no Beauty.

Only the undreamt dream knows significance,
Only the vision we do not see has essential form;
Beauty is a vision imperfectly seen,
Beauty is the sound our ears hear only partly.

There is a stillness in the heart of sound.
Let me escape into that stillness
Which is Nothing and Everything;
Let me escape from the sharp pain of Beauty
For Beauty is a sword that pierces the heart;
Then shall I be the End and the Beginning,
Then shall I be Myself and Everyone
And also No one.
Beauty will not exist . . .

Beauty is here and now,
It is not hereafter. . . .

The Water Flows

THE water flows
Peacefully along . . .
Under the trees
Like a song
Unsung.

Peacefully the water flows
Under the trees,
Brown water deep and cool,
Like beautiful words
That no one has said.
For the lips that might have spoken them
Are dead,
But the words are there still
In the stream,
Carried along
With the silent song . . .

Gentle winding stream
Under the trees,
You are like a dream
That might have been dreamt

But the dreamer awoke
Too soon . . .
The dream is here
In the stream,
Carried along
With the song
And the words
That are too lovely to be said.

The stream ripples and murmurs,
It talks as it flows,
But it is not the stream that I hear,
It is the deep dream and the song and the
      rhythm of beautiful words.
They are there
Under the trees
Flowing along . . .
O song,
O words,
O dream,
You do not only *seem,*
You are there in the deep reality of final peace.

The Sculptor

In silence beauty will take form and grow . . .
In silence, in a dark place will beauty stand
Deathless—eternal—with an outstretched hand.
Soft! Do not frighten her—tread gently—so . . .
Pile up the lumps of sticky common clay,
Tools of your trade, tools that you understand,
Mould, shape and build with ever-loving hand,
Be swift—be swift—for beauty will not stay.

And at the end? The sculptured stone—who'll buy?
Some rich man, proud of purse and flair;
"Fine piece of work! 'Twill give the place an air."
How shall he understand your desperate sigh:
Not this, I saw—not this.
On rubbish heap, discarded clay says—Why?
I that once lived for beauty's kiss
And now, discarded, on an ashpit lie.

So why?—I ask—
Why have I lived?
From me was beauty formed.
And now
Oh why—oh why?

A Wandering Tune

HAIR like a mist and eyes so wide apart and grey
That do not smile
But look far out as though they see
Once in a while
Things that Humanity,
The rank and file,
Shall never glimpse—they are so far away.
There in the crowded street they see
The desert sands and sometimes hear
An endless tune, now far, now near.

The piper pipes. The wandering tune
Floats out and upward to the moon
And stirs the palm trees in the breeze
And stirs the heart that listens yet . . .
Oh, wandering tune that wakes again
Forgotten longing and dead pain
And will not let the heart forget.
Oh, wandering tune
Beneath the moon,
Now far, now near—
That endless tune
Beneath the moon.

Places

Ctesiphon

SPEAK softly, let me sit and, dreaming, see
A golden arch uprising to the skies,
See it so clearly through my closed eyes
That, once again, I stand there quietly . . .
There, where Men built for glory, there shall be
Only bare beauty left, unheeding, wise,
Scornful of Midget Man who wars and dies,
Who builds and toils and suffers endlessly . . .

There shall remain at last the crumbling clay,
The loneliness of naked beauty bared,
The wild birds flying forth from sanctuary . . .
Let me remember one enchanted day . . .
And all the loveliness of beauty shared.
Speak softly, let me sit and, dreaming, see.

In Baghdad

GREEN
Green melons
Round
Oblong
Numbers piled up
Green and round . . .
Innocent round melons saying nothing,
Nothing at all.
In the corner there are melons gashed and split
With naked pink flesh
And thousands of flies settling on them.
Thousands of flies
Ugh!

God sees the world like a round green melon,
And then he sees the flies
Buzzing and settling . . .
But, being merciful,
He looks away and says,
"I will try not to think of these human beings . . ."
Allah is very merciful.

An Island

I HAVE sat dreaming in a quiet place . . .
The green leaves met above my head,
A river rustled in its bed,
And all around
Was sweet and stealthy woodland sound.
Such was a bower within the wood
To fit a hidden secret mood . . .
And yet my eyes looked out and saw
Not the dark sweetness of the wood
But far off misty hills of blue
Seen from a hillside where there grew
Genista flowers and Iris white
(Do you remember our delight?)
And from that hillside where we lay
On that thrice blessed halcyon day
We saw—above all mortal ills
The misty everlasting hills . . .
"I will lift up mine eyes and see—"
And dream that you are there with me.

The Nile

Do you remember water like molten silver gleaming?
And white sails that crept slowly past?
Stealthily, silently, as though they knew
They might disturb our sweet enchanted dreaming . . .
My heart, that night, was silent too
Or did it stir? Stir and awake from its long dreaming?
It was so quiet that I scarcely knew . . .

I only know next morn the sands were golden
And that day broke for us alone.
It came and brought us joy—and now is gone.
But there remain in that enchanted land
Our footprints in the golden endless sand . . .

Dartmoor

I SHALL not return again the way I came,
Back to the quiet country where the hills
Are purple in the evenings, and the tors
Are grey and quiet, and the tall standing stones
Lead out across the moorland till they end
At water's edge.
It is too gentle, all that land,
It will bring back
Such quiet dear remembered things,
There, where the longstone lifts its lonely head,
Gaunt, grey, forbidding,
Ageless, however worn away;
There, even, grows the heather . . .
Tender, kind,
The little streams are busy in the valleys,
The rivers meet by the grey Druid bridge,
So quiet,
So quiet,
Not as death is quiet, but as life can be quiet
When it is sweet.

To a Cedar Tree

Do you remember Lebanon?
The stillness and the snows?
The cool cold glare
And a blue sky—pitiless—
Or sometimes grey and heavy with unfallen snow?

In the summers that were of polished brown hills
(But always the stillness—the mountain tops)
Here Solomon's men came to hew and fell the cedars
And the trees were taken to stand
Proudly in the temple of God . . .

But they had been nearer to God,
Had lived with God in the hills,
Had whispered to God in the stillness;
They had been proud then and unafraid.

And you, my Cedar tree, in my garden by the Thames,
Brought in a ship and planted in a strange land
Near to the river
With farm lands all around,
Close to the toil and the labour of men,

Stately you grew, your branches wide,
Gracious you stand
With smooth clipped lawn all around you

And an English herbaceous border
Flaunting its bloom on a summer's day.
You are a part of England now:
"Tea will be served on the lawn
Under the Cedar tree."

But do you remember Lebanon?
Beloved tree—do you remember Lebanon?

Calvary

On Calvary, in midday's burning heat,
What thoughts in Mary's heart, as pale she stands?
What echoed words, remembered words, that beat
From out the past, and make her clench her hands?
Gold, frankincense and myrrh . . . The Sages kneel,
And simple shepherds all agog with joy,
With Angels praising God who doth reveal
His love for men in Christ, the newborn boy . . .

Where now the incense? Where the kingly gold?
For Jesus only bitter myrrh and woe.
Here hangs no kingly figure—just a son
In pain and dying . . .

                        How shall Mary know
That with his sigh: " *'Tis finished . . .*" all is told?
Then—at *that* moment—Christ's Reign has begun!

Love Poems and Others

Count Fersen to the Queen

In the North the snows are falling,
In the North the birds are calling,
But my heart that lives for loving
    Shall not hear its mate reply.

In the North white streams are flowing,
In the North the flowers are blowing,
But my heart that is a lover's
    Shall not know a second Spring . . .

Hers the ring upon my finger,
Now I pray may death not linger,
Say of me "He was a Lover,"
    Lived and died to serve a Queen.

Beatrice Passes

WHERE she passes, there is Light
After Night. . . .
A smile that follows on a sigh
As she goes by. . . .
With her footsteps comes a sound
All round,
As of wild and woodland things
Gently stirring fragile things
　　　When Beatrice passes by. . . .

With her presence comes a calm
Full of balm. . . .
Where she steps the flowers abound
On holy ground. . . .
At her touch the trembling trees,
Even these,
Put forth tender buds that break,
Blossoming for her sweet sake
　　　Who is Light and Love. . . .

At her coming there is Life
After strife!

Larks are singing in the sky
When she draws nigh!
At her voice the quivering Earth
Knows rebirth,
Stirs me to a sudden cry!
 Then she passes—passes by,
Leaving (so to me it seems)
Only darkness filled with dreams. . . .

Undine

UNDINE, straight and gold and white . . .
Shimmering tresses, braided bright . . .
Lips, not scarlet—Scarlet? No,
Cool and pale as water's flow.
Cool and pale against my heart
All thy body, and thou art
Like a lily on the lake
Where no man his thirst shall slake.
And thy petals tightly curled
Hold the jewel of the world,
Looking in thy deep green eyes
Far I see it where it lies
Hidden by the water's play,
Grave sweet soul behind the gay.

Now I know no jewel's there
So forever thou art fair . . .
So forever,
Loving never,
Thou art fair, Undine,
So fair . . .
Unforgettably, so fair . . .

Hawthorn Trees in Spring

A Lament of Women

How heavy are the hawthorn trees,
Weighed down with blossom,
Laden with heavy perfume,
Like the bodies and souls of women
Heavy with fruit of men's desire
Or with their own desire in Spring.

Up in the sky, divorced from earth,
The aeroplanes pass
Roaring along on their gallant adventures;
They are the souls of men
Set free from earth,
Set free from the load of blossom
And the cloying perfumes of Spring,
They fly and are free.

Yet at the last they must return,
Fall back to earth,
Gliding down presently and skimming the ground

Or falling in vivid flame,
Yet still returning to earth.

And there shall Earth
Gather them once again in her inmost womb
And in due course
The trees shall be laden again
With leaves and blossom and fruit.
How heavy are the hawthorn trees . . .
How heavy . . . how achingly sweet.
Shall there never be peace?
And cold clear air?
With never a scent or a breath
Of the growing clustering flowering earth?
How heavy are the hawthorn trees in Spring,
How painfully, achingly sweet . . .

The Lament of the Tortured Lover

I HAVE *said* I adore you;
I have said it—I have said it.
Said it against your throat
Where the pulses beat
And under the curve of your breast . . .

Outside the moon rides high in the sky,
A lemon moon,
A moon the colour of honey
Made by the bees from lime trees.
O pale lemon-coloured moon,
You were worshipped five thousand years ago,
The temples they built you are dust
Or buried under the earth,
But you are still the moon
Riding high and proud in the sky . . .

I am sick of words
Of everlasting meaningless words.
I love you—I love you—that parrot cry.
Cannot flesh take flesh in silence?
But no—you will not have it so.

You were made for incense,
For burning words,
Words—words—words—going on through the night . . .
While I worship the pulse in your throat
And the curve of your breast . . .
In twenty years your face will be haggard,
Your eyes will be cold,
Your sagging breasts will not stir my desire—
But the moon will be still the moon . . .

And I?
What am I?
I am a man who loves you
Desperately, blindly.
I am a man in the street
Seeing the moon . . .
I am an old man in a club
Ringing the bell and saying "Old brandy."
I am curled up in my mother's womb
Knowing nothing of all this extraordinary business
Called Life,
Unhurt by the torture of beauty,
Unconscious as yet that beauty is . . .
I am all these things and always have been
And ever shall be.

O moon, ride high in the sky tonight,
Ride high,
Ride high. . . .

What Is Love?

LOVE is a white flame—And a smouldering smoky fire
It is a green tree—And a grey cathedral spire
Love is an ecstasy—pure—It stirs in mud and slime
It is youth and delight—It is cold and sublime
There is none shall say
What Love is—or is not,
And which of us shall say:
"Dwell!" or "Depart!"
Love will not stay
And will not leave the heart
At our desire or plea.
But oh! for me
This would I pray
That Love might be a tree
Rooted in time—for all eternity.

To M.E.L.M. in Absence

Now is the winter past, but for my part
Still winter stays until we meet again.
Dear love, I have your promise and your heart
But lacking touch and sight, spring buds bring pain.
Friendship is ours, and still in absence grows.
No dearer friend I own, so close, so kind.
Knowledge is yours, from you to me it flows
And I have loved your wise and gentle mind.
Beauty we share, a white magnolia tree
Rooted in England brings you to my side
And Roman columns rising from the sea
Must surely bring remembrance with the tide.

    So in my winter, love, I dream of spring
    Enclosed within the circle of your ring . . . .

Remembrance

IF I should leave you in the days to come—
God grant that may not be—
But yet if so,
Your love for me must fade I know.
You will remember—and you will forget.
But oh! imperishable—strong
My love for you shall burn and glow
Deep in your heart—your whole life long,
Unknown, unseen, but living still in bliss
So you shall bear me with you all the days.
Forget then what you will.
I died—but not my love for you,
That lives for aye—though dumb,
Remember this
If I should leave you in the days to come.

A Choice

I AM tired of the past that clings around my feet,
I am tired of the past that will not let life be sweet,
I would cut it away with a knife and say
Let me be myself—reborn—today.

But I am afraid of the past—that it will creep back to my feet
And look in my face and say, "You laugh and eat
But I am here with you yet . . .
You would not remember—but I will not let you forget . . ."
What is or is not courage? Who shall say?
Shall I be brave or base if I cut the past away?

Sometimes I have dreamed that you have stood and said:
"I too have sometimes longed to be freed from the dead
Burden of our remembrance, free from your sorrow."
Let there be no yesterday and no tomorrow,
Let there be for us only today,
Ride it—ride it through Time and away.

My Flower Garden

THERE is no knowing
What time shall bring,
What then is growing
This day of Spring?

Love that is lonely,
Love far away,
Ah! could I only
See you for a day.

Love-that-lies-bleeding
And love-in-the-mist,
Tulips that need you
Still staying unkist.

You are my heart, love,
And you are my life,
We are apart, love,
And I am your wife.

God then have pity
And bring you to me

Here in the city
From over the sea.

When you come home, love,
What words will there be?
You will say "Sunflower"
And say it to me.

Enchantment

I LOST my love, she left me.
My fair love,
My false love,
My fair false love.

I wandered to the Fairy Hills,
I cried to them to mend my ills,
I called to my lost love,
My fair love, my false love.
I saw a Fairy Lady there
With long white hands and drowning hair . . .
And oh!—her face was wild and sweet,
Was sweet and wild,
Was wild and strange and fair . . .

Her eyes looked past me,
Through me and beyond me,
Seeking for a vanished Fairy Lover.
I walked by her side there,
Down a Fairy Ride there,
Seeking for a vanished Fairy Lover.
I cried to the Hills there

That they should mend my ills there,
I called to my lost love,
My fair love, my false fair love.

But the Fairy Lady by my side
She neither spoke nor moaned nor cried
But pushed aside her drowning hair
And oh! her face was wild and sweet
And sweet and wild and fair . . .

And now I am at home again
And many seek to ease my pain
They say in time I shall forget
My fair love,
My false love,
My fair false love . . .

And no one knows to look at me
That all the time I only see
Two long white hands and drowning hair
And oh! a face so wild and strange and fair . . .

Jenny by the Sky

(*From* Star over Bethlehem)

Come down to me, Jenny, come down from the hill,
Come down to me here where I wait,
Come down to my arms, to my lips, my desire,
Come down all my hunger to sate.

But Jenny walks lonely, her head in the air,
She walks on the hilltop, the wind in her hair,
She will not come down to me, loud though I cry,
She walks with the wind, upturned face to the sky . . .

In the cool of the evening I walked in the glade,
And there I met God . . . and I was not afraid.
Together we walked in the depths of the wood
And together we looked at the things we had made,
Together we looked—and we saw they were good . . .

God made the World and the stars set on high,
The Galaxies rushing, none knows where or why.
God fashioned the Cosmos, the Universe wide,

And the hills and the valleys, the birds in the wood,
God made them and loved them, and saw they were good . . .

And I—have made Jenny! To walk on the hill.
She will not come down to me loud though I cry;
She walks there for ever, her face to the sky,
She will not come down though I call her,
She will not come down to my greed,
She is as I dreamed her . . . and made her
Of my loving and longing and need . . .

With my mind and my heart I made Jenny,
I made her of love and desire,
I made her to walk on the hilltop
In loneliness, beauty and fire . . .

In the cool of the evening I walked in the wood
And God walked beside me . . .
We both understood.

Verses of Nowadays

From a Grown-up to a Child

THE fairies talk to little girls,
They push aside their golden curls
And whisper in a shell-pink ear—
But what they say *we* cannot hear.
We grown-ups are so tall and proud
And fairies *hate* to shout aloud.

The fairies run along the ground
And baby girls can hear the sound,
They double up, and crow and kick
And beg their mothers to look quick.
But when we look, they've always past,
The little fairies run so fast.

The fairies stay awake all night
So little girls need take no fright,
For if the night light *does* go out
They know the fairies are about,
And they can hear their silky wings—
They *are* so kind, these darling things!

I Wore My New Canary Suit

I WORE my new canary suit
To go and meet my love,
We talked and talked of everything
In earth and heaven above.

I went again to meet my love,
The years had flitted by,
I wore my old canary suit
To bid my love goodbye.

I took it to a jumble sale
But brought it back once more
And hung it on an inner peg
Within my cupboard door.

I shall not meet my love again
For he is in his grave.
So—I've an old moth-eaten suit
And he is young and brave. . . .

Racial Musings

PRESUMPTIVE is Man to claim the right
To arbitrate between God's creatures so
And place a gulf between the Black and White
Deeper than sea or ocean waters flow.
So strange it seems, this unpigmented pride,
The paleness of a skin that knows not sun . . .
Men all are built of bone;
How hard then to decide
If they are Apes or Men
When life is done!

Some think, and more than one,
That coffee-coloured children meet the case,
It is our duty so to take one's fun
That the resulting mixture has a face
That nicely illustrates Mendelian lore.
Oh, coffee-coloured world,
You'll be a BORE.
Satiety but no variety.
A BORE. A BORE. A BORE.

Picnic 1960

AFTERNOON Tea by the side of the road
That is the meal that I love,
Hundreds of cars rushing past all the time,
Sunshine and clouds up above!

Get out the chairs and set up the tea,
Serviettes, too, are a must.
Never a moment that's quiet or dull,
Sausage rolls flavoured with dust!

Time to go home? Strew the orange peel round,
Leave paper and portions of pie,
Pack up the crocks and get into the queue,
Perfect picnic place, love, and goodbye . . .

The *Agatha Christie* Collection

THE HERCULE POIROT MYSTERIES

Match your wits with the famous Belgian detective.

Explore more at www.AgathaChristie.com

The *Agatha Christie* Collection

THE MISS MARPLE MYSTERIES

Join the legendary spinster sleuth from
St. Mary Mead in solving murders far and wide.

The Murder at the Vicarage

The Body in the Library

The Moving Finger

A Murder Is Announced

They Do It with Mirrors

A Pocket Full of Rye

4:50 From Paddington

The Mirror Crack'd

A Caribbean Mystery

At Bertram's Hotel

Nemesis

Sleeping Murder

Miss Marple: The Complete
Short Story Collection

THE TOMMY AND TUPPENCE MYSTERIES

Jump on board with the entertaining crime-solving
couple from Young Adventurers Ltd.

The Secret Adversary

Partners in Crime

N or M?

By the Pricking of My Thumbs

Postern of Fate

Explore more at www.AgathaChristie.com

The
Agatha Christie
Collection

Don't miss a single one of Agatha Christie's stand-alone novels and short-story collections.

Agatha Christie™

See your favorite detectives come to life on screen!

These and other DVDs and
downloads available now at:

www.acornonline.com